‘You’ve got e  contract elsew
‘But I’d be ve
would give me

Jane held her br her whole future depended on what Lyall said now.

‘On two conditions,’ he said at last.

‘What are they?’

‘First, that there’s no repetition of your behaviour this morning,’ said Lyall astringently. ‘I expect the people I work with to behave like professionals.’

Jane steeled herself for the rest of it. ‘And the second condition?’

‘That you have dinner with me tonight.’

Dear Reader

Welcome to our exciting mini-series—**Sealed with a Kiss**. Every month we'll be featuring a romance sparked off by a letter, an advertisement, or even a diary. Some of the world's greatest romances have begun in writing...and ended with a marriage licence! This is a tradition continued by ten of our popular authors—each and every one of whom has brought her own unique style to the romance.

We hope that you enjoy this **Sealed with a Kiss** title and all the other terrific romances that we have out this month!

The Editor

P.S. Look out for next month's **Sealed with a Kiss** title - THE BEST FOR LAST by Stephanie Howard

LEGALLY BINDING

BY
JESSICA HART

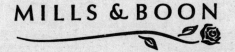

MILLS & BOON

All the characters in this book have no existence outside the imagination of the author, and have no relation whatsoever to anyone bearing the same name or names. They are not even distantly inspired by any individual known or unknown to the author, and all the incidents are pure invention.

MILLS & BOON and the Rose Device
are trademarks of the publisher.
Harlequin Mills & Boon Limited,
Eton House, 18-24 Paradise Road, Richmond, Surrey TW9 1SR
This edition published by arrangement with
Harlequin Enterprises B.V.

© Jessica Hart 1995

ISBN 0 263 79046 0

Set in Times Roman 10 on 11¼ pt.
01-9507-59010 C1

Made and printed in Great Britain

PROLOGUE

Miss Jane Makepeace
Makepeace and Son
Penbury Road
Starbridge
Gloucestershire

Dear Miss Makepeace

I am writing to draw your attention to the fact that, as at the close of business tonight, your current account was overdrawn £897, which exceeds your agreed facility of £500.

Recent accounts have shown discouraging figures for Makepeace and Son, and in the circumstances I feel that it would be advisable for us to meet to discuss your financial situation. If your business prospects show no signs of an imminent recovery, the bank will have to consider carefully its current investment in your firm.

I would be grateful if you would telephone my secretary to arrange a time to come in and see me at the earliest possible opportunity.

Yours sincerely,

DEREK OWEN
Business Banking Manager

Makepeace and Son
Starbridge, Gloucestershire

Chairman & Chief Executive
Multiplex Plc
Multiplex House
LONDON EC1

Dear Sir

We have pleasure in submitting herewith our tender for the initial stages of the restoration work on Penbury Manor which we hope will meet with your favourable consideration.

Makepeace and Son is a local firm with a well-established reputation for quality and value. We are sure that you will appreciate the advantages of having a team of highly skilled craftsmen ready to start work at the earliest possible opportunity. Our current commitments are such that we would be able to concentrate exclusively on the restoration of Penbury Manor and we are confident that we would be able to meet the proposed completion date three months early.

We offer exceptional value, the prestige of true craftsmanship and the reassurance of a quality of service that is second to none. In addition, I can, as Managing Director, assure you of my personal attention at all times throughout the execution of the work.

I very much hope to have the opportunity of working in partnership with you on the restoration of this lovely old house.

Yours faithfully

JANE MAKEPEACE
Managing Director

CHAPTER ONE

THERE was a storm on the way.

'About time,' muttered Jane to herself, glancing at the black clouds boiling up in the distance as she snipped off another spray of roses. The gardens were bone-dry, and everyone had been on edge for days now, waiting for the oppressive heat to break. It hadn't made the interminable wait for news about the contract any easier. A big storm to clear the air was just what they all needed.

Thunder grumbled behind the rolling wolds, but Jane wasn't inclined to hurry. It still sounded some way away, and she didn't often get the chance to escape like this. It was very hot, and in the eerie pre-storm stillness the fragrance of the roses smothering the old stone wall somehow intensified. Jane loved these times, alone in the neglected garden, with only the empty manor house for company. She could clear her mind of all her worries about Kit and the business and what would happen if they didn't get the contract to restore the manor, and submerge herself in the beauty of the garden instead, dreaming impossible dreams of what might have been if Miss Partridge hadn't moved out of the manor. If her father hadn't died. If Kit were different.

If she had gone with Lyall all those years ago.

Jane clamped down on the thought. She didn't allow herself to think about Lyall, and if anyone had asked she would have said that she never did. It was only at times like this when she was alone or tired or off guard that the memories would uncurl dangerously inside her and the feel of him tingled still over her skin.

Lyall...would she never be rid of him? Jane shook herself irritably and stepped round a clump of lupins to cut some Belle de Crécy. They were Miss Partridge's favourites, and she buried her nose in the deep pink roses to banish unwelcome memories in their rich, spicy scent.

'Hello, Jane.'

Jane froze, her face still bent over the roses. The voice behind her sounded so like Lyall's that she had the uncanny feeling that her thoughts had conjured him out of the past, and she had to tell herself sternly not to be ridiculous. The edgy pre-storm atmosphere was simply making her imagine things. It had been ten years since she had heard that deep, lazily good-humoured voice, nine years since she had stopped hoping ever to hear it again and started trying to forget.

'Jane?'

Very slowly, Jane lifted her head from the roses. It's not Lyall, she reassured herself, and turned, only to squeeze her eyes shut against the dizzying sensation of plummeting through time, through ten long, empty years.

Lyall Harding, the man who had swept into her life, turning everything upside-down, the man who had taught her about laughter and about love, the man whose smile had haunted her dreams ever since he had walked away that grey September day ten years ago. How could he be standing on the worn brick path looking exactly the same?

Half convinced that her mind was playing tricks on her for some reason, Jane opened her eyes cautiously, but he was still there, still looking *exactly* the same. The same amusement glinting in the navy blue eyes, the same mobile mouth, the same air of suppressed energy.

Lyall smiled the same devastating smile. 'Remember me?' he said.

Remember him? How could she forget her first lover, her only lover? How many times had she wished that she could? Jane felt jarred, disorientated, ricocheting helplessly between panic, fury and despair at the wild, irresistible joy that surged through her in spite of all those years of telling herself that she didn't care and didn't remember and wouldn't want to see him even if he did come back.

'Hello, Lyall,' she croaked, hating herself for sounding in her turn exactly like the breathless teenager she had been ten years ago.

'So you do remember!' The mockery that had always so unsettled her gleamed in his eyes. 'I was beginning to think you were going to ignore me completely.'

'I wasn't expecting you,' said Jane, in what must have been the understatement of the century. She was still clutching the secateurs in one hand and the trug full of roses in the other, and her grey eyes were wide and very wary.

'I recognised you straight away,' he said, and gestured up to the terrace behind him. 'You were standing there, bending your head to smell the roses, and your eyes were closed. It was just as I remembered you,' he added in a curious voice. 'You haven't changed at all.'

Jane took a deep breath and reminded herself that she was no longer a susceptible teenager. She was sensible, practical Jane Makepeace who had learnt her lesson about Lyall's charm a long time ago.

'Yes, I have,' she said, relieved to hear how steady her voice sounded. 'I've changed a lot. I'm not nineteen any longer.'

'It doesn't show,' he assured her. 'Your hair's still the colour of smooth, dark honey, your eyes are still the clearest grey—and you still put up your prickles when you're caught unawares.'

Prickles instantly alert, Jane eyed him resentfully. Lyall had always had such a vivid, unsettling presence that no one ever noticed that he wasn't nearly as handsome as he seemed at first. His face was too lean, his nose too big, but it was the air of reckless charm that people remembered, she thought. She should know. She had been trying to forget it for ten years. 'It doesn't sound as if you've changed either,' she said tartly. 'Still the same old line!'

Lyall looked back at her. 'It worked before,' he reminded her.

It had. Treacherous colour crept up Jane's throat and stained her cheeks as she remembered how completely she had succumbed to his charm before. She had always hated her obstinately straight, silky hair but Lyall used to love it—or say that he did, she remembered bitterly. He would spread it out and watch it shine in the light as it slid through his fingers.

The blue eyes watching her gleamed with sardonic amusement. She was standing in the middle of the border, surrounded by flowers, holding the trug in front of her in an unconsciously defensive gesture while the afternoon sun, slanting between the dark clouds, spun a golden haze around her. Jane tried very hard to look cool and unconcerned by his survey, but she had the disconcerting feeling that he knew exactly what she was thinking about, just as he had always done in the past.

'Aren't you going to come out of there?' he asked.

Jane didn't want to come out. She didn't want to stand next to him and remember how it felt to touch him. She wanted to stay right where she was among the roses, protected by their thorns, but Lyall would know that too, of course.

She told herself not to be pathetic. She was twenty-nine, not an impressionable teenager, and Lyall was just an old acquaintance who meant nothing to her any more.

Tilting her chin unconsciously, she edged between the iceberg roses and a gorgeous clump of peonies that were past their best, and stretched over a mass of wild geraniums so wide that she nearly lost her balance and would have fallen if Lyall hadn't reached out and caught her by the arm to steady her as she landed on the grass.

At the touch of his hand against her bare skin, Jane's stomach disappeared beneath an avalanche of memories: those same hands sliding up her arms, pulling her towards him, gentling down her spine. The feel of his body, the touch of his lips, the warmth of his smile...

She caught her breath and jerked her arm from Lyall's grasp. Not daring to look at him, certain that her memories were written all over her face, she bent her head over the trug, resetting the flowers with unsteady fingers.

Lyall meant nothing to her now, *remember*?

Steeling herself, Jane looked up. His eyes were as blue and as dark as ever, but instead of the laughter she remembered they held an expression she had never seen before. Gone was the glinting mockery, and in its place was something harder, something fixed and almost fierce that dried the breath in her throat and set her heart knocking painfully against her ribs.

He *had* changed. She could see that now that she was close to him. There was a steely solidity about him now, a toughness that she didn't remember, and new lines starred beneath his eyes. She didn't remember that ruthless look to his mouth, either, she realised. It was as if the wild recklessness and carefree independence that had been so much a part of him had focused itself into a harder, more daunting quality of power and authority.

Unprepared for the transformation, Jane stared, only to see that strange expression dissolve and the mouth which had suddenly seemed so inflexible curl up at one corner, and she took a hurried step back, furious with herself. She was supposed to be keeping her dignity and treating him like a stranger, not gazing into his eyes as if she had been waiting for him for ten years.

Scarlet-cheeked, she took a firm grip on her trug and on herself. 'I didn't think we'd ever see *you* again,' she said as coolly as she could.

'Life's full of surprises, isn't it?' A disconcerting smile lurked at the back of the blue eyes and Jane fought the instinctive urge to respond. She had succumbed to Lyall's smile too often in the past, and look where it had got her!

'Not always nice ones,' she pointed out in an attempt to sound quelling, but she might as well have spared her breath.

'You don't sound very pleased to see me, Jane!' said Lyall, without appearing unduly concerned.

'Did you think I would be?' she retorted with a challenging look.

Lyall considered the matter. 'Why not? We had some good times together, didn't we?'

Jane had tried so hard to forget those times. 'It's the bad times I remember,' she said bleakly.

'I don't remember any bad times,' he said.

'You must have a very selective memory,' said Jane, beginning to walk back to the terrace. 'Or have you forgotten how we parted all those years ago?'

'No, I haven't forgotten.' Without appearing to hurry, Lyall kept up with her easily. 'But that was different. I was thinking about the times we spent together, not the time we spent apart. Don't you ever remember them?'

Oh, how she remembered! She remembered everything: the exhilaration bubbling along her veins, the shivery joy of being with him, the feeling of being drenched in sunlight. 'I try not to,' she said.

'Why not?'

Jane's lips tightened. That was typical Lyall. He could never let anything go. She remembered how easily he used to be able to tie her up in knots with his arguments until he had somehow proved that she was wrong and she was utterly confused about what she thought. Now he wanted her to admit that her happiness with him had been so intense that she couldn't bear to remember it. Well, she wasn't going to! Stopping short, she swung round to face him. 'What are you doing here, Lyall?' she demanded.

'Just having a look around.' Unperturbed by the abrupt change of subject, Lyall glanced around the overgrown garden and up to Penbury Manor. Dating back to the fifteenth century, it had grown in a haphazardly graceful way, acquiring extra wings and gables which had added to rather than detracted from its mellow charm. With the afternoon sun turning its warm stone golden, it stood silhouetted against the blue-black storm clouds like an elaborate film set. 'This old place hasn't changed much either, has it?'

'It's about to,' said Jane with some bitterness, although she was glad enough to keep the conversation on neutral ground.

'Oh?'

'Miss Partridge couldn't manage here any more, so she had to sell. Some ghastly high-tech company is going to ruin it by turning it into an office and building a research laboratory in the rose garden.'

Lyall assumed an expression of outrage and threw up his hands in mock-protest. 'Not the rose garden!'

'It's not funny! It takes years to create a garden like that. All it needs is some care and it could be beautiful again, but this company isn't interested in beauty. The roses interfere with its neat, tidy plot, so they're going to rip them up and burn them!'

'Still the same old Jane,' mocked Lyall, a faint edge to his voice. 'You always did care more about plants than about people, didn't you?'

'That's not true!' Jane marched up the steps to the terrace as the sun was abruptly swallowed up by a billowing black bank of cloud and the thunder rolled ominously close.

'Isn't it? I seem to remember that you were much nicer to flowers than you were to me.'

'At least I always knew where I was with plants!'

'What do you mean by that?'

But Jane was already regretting saying as much. The first heavy drops of rain were already splattering on to the terrace and she had no intention of getting into an argument with Lyall. He was a stranger now, and that was how she wanted to keep it. 'Does it matter?' she said, proud of her own self-control. 'It's going to pour. If you want to stand around arguing about the past, that's up to you, but as far as I'm concerned it's not worth getting wet, so I'm afraid we'll have to cut the reminiscences.' The heavens opened as she spoke, and, grateful for the excuse, she shouted what she hoped was a cool goodbye before she began to run. Eyes screwed up against the downpour, she didn't look back, and her shoes crunched over the gravel at the front of the house. It wasn't far, but the rain was so heavy that she was drenched and breathless by the time she reached the old van with Makepeace and Son painted proudly on its side.

Jane practically threw the trug in the back and banged the door shut against the rain and against Lyall, but the next instant the passenger door opened and he got in beside her, running his hand through his wet hair. Jane froze in the act of wiping the wetness from her cheeks and looked at him in outrage. 'I don't remember offering you a lift!'

Lyall didn't appear the slightest bit bothered by the hostility of his reception. 'You can't really mean to drive off and leave me standing out in this, can you?' He nodded up at the roof where the rain was drumming with a tropical fury, and thunder rolled menacingly as if to underline the inhumanity of the idea.

'Why can't you get into your own car?' she asked accusingly.

'Because I left it in the village and walked up here,' he said. 'Any objections?'

His plain white T-shirt was sticking damply to the powerfully muscled shoulders, and as his eyes dropped from her face to her chest Jane realised that her own sleeveless cotton shirt was clinging equally revealingly. The quick colour rose in her face, and she plucked at the wet material crossly in an effort to make her curves a little less obvious.

'You shouldn't be here anyway,' she grumbled, unnerved by the knowing look in his eyes. What was it about him that set her so on edge? To everyone else she was a model of cool practicality, but Lyall only had to look at her and she was a flustered teenager all over again. 'This is private property, in case you'd forgotten.'

'You're here.'

'I've got permission to be here,' she pointed out.

'From the "ghastly company"?'

'From the estate agents,' said Jane coldly. 'I can come and pick flowers for Miss Partridge until the company takes possession. I hardly think they'd want people like you poking around.'

'In that case you'd better make sure I leave by giving me a lift back to the village,' said Lyall with an odd glinting look. 'If they've been generous enough to let you swipe all their flowers, I'd have thought it was the least you could do.'

'It's the least I can do,' he had said, leaning across the seat to open the car door. 'I'm going into Starbridge anyway. Come on, get in.'

Jane hesitated, and Lyall's eyes glinted with amused understanding. 'Don't say that you've been warned against me already?'

She had. She had had quite enough time since he had knocked her off her bike that day to discover that Lyall Harding meant trouble. He was wild, he was reckless, and it was uniformly agreed in the village that he would come to no good. The girls in the district might have brightened at the rumour that he had come back after a mysterious eight-year absence, but their parents had wasted no time in warning them against him. Jane's own father had been horrified to hear that his daughter had been one of the first to meet Lyall after his return. 'You don't want anything more to do with him,' he had said. 'Lyall Harding's a maverick. He's never fitted in around here and he never will.'

Jane could believe it. Lyall Harding was like no one she had ever met in her safe, quiet Penbury life. There was a quality of electric excitement about him, a vigour and an unpredictability that made everyone else look a little dim and dull in comparison, and she had been unnerved by its impact as he'd helped her up from the verge where she had landed, winded but unhurt, when she'd wobbled off her bike.

No, she didn't want anything to do with Lyall Harding. Jane was a sensible girl—everyone said so—and sensible girls knew better than to make fools of themselves over men with dancing blue eyes and heart-shaking smiles.

In later years, she wondered how different her life would have been if the bus had appeared on time that day. But it was late, and there was no shelter from the drizzle, and since he was going to Starbridge anyway... So Jane put up her chin in response to the unspoken challenge in his smile and got into the car. If he thought she stood in any danger of succumbing to that dangerous charm, he had another think coming!

He drove much too fast, but his hands were utterly steady on the wheel. Jane clutched at her seat, tense and yet conscious of a deep, unsettling excitement. The firm's van barely managed more than a trundle—rather like her life, she realised with a sudden pang. She was only nineteen; wasn't she too young to be pootling along in the slow lane of life? Lyall probably lived his whole life in top gear.

'I hear you're a good girl,' he said with a sidelong glance as they raced along the narrow country lanes. 'Are you?'

'That depends what you mean by good,' said Jane warily.

'Everyone says how *nice* Jane Makepeace is,' he explained, almost as if he had sensed her momentary dissatisfaction. 'Jane looks after her brother, Jane's nice to old ladies, Jane never gives her father a moment's worry... you can't really be that sensible!'

'What's wrong with being sensible?'

'Nothing,' said Lyall. 'Nothing if you're middle-aged, that is. But you're not, are you, Jane?' He glanced at her again, noting the silky hair and the sweep of her lashes against her skin. 'You must have been a little girl when I left or I'd have noticed you, so you can't be more than eighteen now.'

Jane folded her arms defensively. 'Nineteen.'

'Oh, *that* old?' She hated the laughter in his voice. She guessed that he was about twenty-five or twenty-six, but he already had the assurance of an older man. 'It's still too young to be boring and sensible. You should be learning how to have fun.'

'I know how to have fun!' Jane protested.

'Do you?' he said sceptically.

'Yes!'

'OK, let's go to the sea and see if the sun's shining there.'

Jane stared at him. 'What, *now*?'

'Why not?'

'I—I can't,' she stammered. 'I've got to do the shopping.'

'We'll do it on the way back.'

'But I can't just disappear for the day! They'll wonder where I am.'

'Ring them and tell them you've met a friend and you'll be late back,' said Lyall. 'Or do you only know how to have fun if you've planned it a week in advance and made sure it's all right with your father?'

Of course, she should have ignored him. She should have told him that she didn't care what he thought about her and insisted that he drop her at the supermarket. Instead she had let him drive her all the way to the sea and the clouds had cleared and the sun had come out.

And so it had begun.

Did Lyall remember? Jane couldn't look at him. She clung to the steering-wheel as if it were an anchor against the tide of memories. Outside the rain beat relentlessly against the windscreen, but in the van the air was taut and tight with tension.

'Why have you come back?' she burst out.

Lyall half turned in his seat so that he could watch her face. 'Why shouldn't I?'

'You've been perfectly happy not to come back for the last ten years,' said Jane, hating the accusing note in her voice.

He shrugged. 'There was no reason for me to come back before,' he said, and his eyes rested for a moment on Jane's mouth. 'Was there?' He might have said that he only remembered the good times, but the bitterness of their last parting still lay bleak and undeniable between them.

Jane kept her eyes on the rain. 'What's the reason now?'

'Oh ... business,' said Lyall vaguely.

'In Penbury? I thought we were all too *small-minded* for you here?' The accusation had rankled for ten years, and it showed in Jane's voice.

'Perhaps I'm hoping that other people will have changed more than you have,' he said, and she flushed. He had always had the ability to put her in the wrong.

'That doesn't explain why you're snooping around Penbury Manor,' she said sharply.

Lyall's expression didn't change, but Jane had the oddest feeling that he was suddenly amused. 'I wasn't snooping,' he said. 'Nor do I have to explain anything to you, but if you must know I happen to have been thinking about the manor recently, and I thought I'd come and look at it again.'

Instinctively, they both peered through the windscreen at the old house. Even shrouded in rain, its jumbled chimneys and leaded windows had a timeless, tranquil beauty. 'Remember how I said I would buy it for you one day?' said Lyall slowly, as if the memory had caught him unawares.

Oh, yes, she remembered. They had been in the woods, looking down on the manor, and the sunlight had thrown dappled shadows on Lyall's face as he'd undone the buttons on her shirt and smiled. That had been the first time they made love, that day when she had thought that his promise meant that she was somehow different from all the other girls he had kissed in Penbury woods. His hands had been so warm and sure against her skin, his mouth so exciting ...

Abruptly Jane reached down and fumbled the key into the ignition. 'It's lucky I didn't hold my breath, isn't it?'

'Just as well,' Lyall agreed calmly, infuriatingly.

Jane reversed jerkily. The past obviously meant nothing to Lyall, so why should she let it bother her? 'Where did you leave your car?'

'At the King's Arms. Do I take it you're going to give me a lift, after all?'

'It doesn't look as if I've got much choice,' said Jane ungraciously as lightning forked outside. 'You're going to have a bad enough time driving back to wherever you came from in this.'

'I'm not driving anywhere,' he said. 'I'm staying at the pub.'

Jane's heart sank. 'Staying?' she echoed in dismay. 'For how long?'

'That depends,' said Lyall. He looked across at Jane. She was leaning forward to frown through the rain, her honey-coloured hair dark and wet and pushed behind her ears. Her face was thinner and more guarded than it had been at nineteen, but her skin was still soft and clear. 'I gather you're running Makepeace and Son now,' he went on after a moment, and the grey eyes flickered briefly towards him.

'How do you know that?' she asked suspiciously.

'I spent last night in the pub,' he said, as if that explained everything. 'From what I heard, you're still busy being the sort of nice, sensible girl who visits old ladies and does the church flowers.'

'You've got no business to ask around about me!' said Jane furiously.

'Oh, come on, Jane, you know what village gossip is like. I didn't even have to ask. All those who remembered me were only too anxious to tell me how much better off you were without me.'

Jane refused to be mollified. 'You used to despise village gossip!'

'I've decided it has its uses,' said Lyall, settling himself more comfortably into his seat. 'For instance, I found out all sorts of interesting things about you that you would probably never have told me yourself.'

'Such as?'

He ignored her sarcasm. 'Such as the fact that you didn't last long in the big bad world. You didn't even finish your first year at horticultural college before you came home.'

'I had to come back,' Jane found herself saying defensively. 'Dad couldn't manage on his own.'

'And like the good girl you were you came running as soon as he called?'

'I suppose if *your* father had had a heart attack you'd have just let him struggle on by himself?'

Lyall's face closed. 'My father was quite capable of looking after himself,' he said with a bitter edge.

'Well, mine wasn't! He needed me to help run the firm while he was ill.'

'Why did it have to be you? Why couldn't your brother do it?'

'Kit was too young.'

'Then, perhaps, but he's not too young now, is he? I heard that he's gone off to South America, leaving you to struggle on with the firm on your own.'

Jane turned out of the drive and concentrated on not letting Lyall get under her skin. 'Kit was at university when Dad died,' she said coldly. 'It was stupid for him not to finish his degree. I'd been helping out in the office since Dad's first heart attack, so I'd learnt how things were run by then. Kit wasn't ready to settle down after he graduated. He wanted to travel, and there was no point in both of us giving up our plans. It made sense for me to carry on by myself.'

'You always did make excuses for Kit,' said Lyall, shaking his head. 'He was the one person you were never sensible about.'

She hadn't been at all sensible about Lyall either, but she could hardly tell him that. 'You never liked Kit,' she accused him instead.

'That's not true,' he said. 'What I didn't like was the way you used to turn yourself into such a martyr for him. You were always worrying about getting back to cook his meals or iron his shirts or clean his shoes.'

'He was just a little boy!'

'He was thirteen—old enough for you to have some life of your own.'

Jane sighed. It was an old argument. Lyall had always resented her closeness to her father, had never understood that she had been looking after her little brother ever since their mother died when she was eleven and that she couldn't just walk away from them.

Lyall himself seemed to realise the futility of arguing about the past. 'So Kit's off in South America, and sensible Jane's stuck in Penbury holding the fort.'

'If you want to put it like that,' she said frostily.

He glanced at her again. 'You were always happiest out in a garden. I can't see you rewiring a house or installing new plumbing.'

'I don't do any of that myself. We employ specialist craftsmen for all the building and restoration work. I just deal with the paperwork and try and find enough work to keep them all busy.'

'Still, it's not exactly what you wanted to do, is it?'

Jane thought of her dreams of finishing the horticultural course one day and setting up as a garden designer. It was all a long way from wrestling with the accounts at Makepeace and Son. 'Not exactly,' she said.

'What's the point of wasting your life doing something you don't want to do?' asked Lyall, just as he had asked all those years ago. 'Your father's dead. You did what you could for him. There's nothing to stop you selling the firm now and going back to gardening.'

'It's not that easy.' The windscreen-wipers slapped desperately at the rain and in the fields the sheep huddled together along the hedgerows in search of some meagre shelter from the downpour. It was dark as a December afternoon, and Jane belatedly remembered to turn on the headlights. 'I can't turn Dorothy and the men out of a job just because I'm fed up.'

'Still making excuses, Jane? Why don't you just admit that you'd rather stay in your nice, safe rut?'

Jane's grey eyes flashed. 'Because it's not true!'

'Isn't it? Why don't you get in a manager if you don't want to sell the firm?'

'Do you think I haven't thought of that?' she said bitterly. 'It's all very well for you to sit there and tell me to do what I want, but we can't all be as selfish and irresponsible as you are! The fact is that I can't afford to pay anyone to do my job at the moment, and, the way things are going, unless we get a big contract soon there won't be a firm left to sell.'

'Is there any chance of that?' Lyall's voice was very casual. It wasn't *his* firm on the line.

'There's a possibility.' Jane hesitated. 'I've tendered for the restoration and rebuilding work at Penbury Manor.'

'What, not the ghastly company that's going to build all over the rose garden?'

She scowled. It might be a joke to him, but it wasn't to her. 'I didn't have much choice,' she said defensively. 'We've got a few small jobs at the moment, but when they've finished I've got nothing to offer the men. I hate the idea of ruining Penbury Manor, but it would give them steady work, and at least I'd be able to stop worrying about money for a while.'

Lyall was watching her with an oddly intent expression. 'So for the time being you're stuck in Penbury?

Still, at least you can't say that you never had the opportunity to escape, can you?'

The narrow space between them jostled with memories. 'Let's go,' Lyall had said. 'We'll go to London, to America, anywhere. There's a big world outside Penbury, Jane. We'll see it together.' His words echoed as if he had shouted them again. Jane stared desperately at the wet road ahead.

'Perhaps I look on it as not having made a terrible mistake,' she said.

'*Is* that how you look at it?'

'Yes,' said Jane firmly, not looking at him, and forgetting all the lonely nights when she had imagined the places she might have seen and the things she might have done if she had gone with Lyall when he'd asked her.

There was a tiny pause. 'Well, as long as you're happy, that's the main thing,' said Lyall lightly.

'Exactly,' she said, relieved that he wasn't going to pursue the subject.

'Are you?'

'Am I what?'

'Happy.'

Jane set her teeth. 'Yes, thank you,' she said tightly, turning a little too sharply down into the village. Lyall probably thought that she had been miserable for the last ten years! 'I'm very happy. Extremely happy, in fact.'

'Apart from the fact that your firm's on the brink of ruin?' To Jane's fury, that hateful undercurrent of laughter was back in his voice.

'I was thinking personally rather than professionally,' she said with a cold look.

'So why haven't you married?' he asked. 'I hear there's been no shortage of suitors. The word in the pub is that you're going out with some solicitor from Starbridge called Eric or something.'

'Alan,' Jane corrected him frostily.

Lyall glanced across at her. 'Is he the reason you're so extremely happy?'

'One of them,' she said, not entirely truthfully. Still, it wouldn't do Lyall any harm to think that there were plenty of men who made her happier than he ever had.

'Why don't you marry him if you're so happy together, then?'

'That's none of your business,' she said in an attempt to sound quelling, but it didn't seem to have much effect on Lyall.

'Still too scared to commit yourself?' he taunted, and Jane stiffened.

'That's good coming from you!'

'I *choose* not to commit myself,' said Lyall. 'And I don't pretend that I ever will. You, on the other hand, used to talk a lot about commitment, but when it came down to it you couldn't bring yourself to take the risk, could you?'

Jane's face tightened as she remembered just why she hadn't gone with Lyall when he had asked her. Had he really forgotten Judith and that terrible argument they had had before he left? 'I had my reasons,' she reminded him bleakly and he looked coolly back at her.

'Yes,' he said. 'The trouble is that they were all the wrong ones.'

It was a relief to reach Penbury at last. A typical Cotswold village, it had a pub facing the green, a poky shop with a post office crammed in one corner, and a fourteenth-century church guarded by an enormous yew tree. Around these three focal points clustered the picturesque cottages built of golden-grey stone, while the newer houses were banished to the fringes of the village, trailing out along the lanes.

Lyall didn't appear to notice the view. He was still watching Jane's face. 'Come and have a drink,' he said as she drew up outside the pub.

'I can't,' she said stiffly. 'I promised I'd go and see Miss Partridge.'

'Later, then?' The momentary coolness had vanished. The dark blue eyes were glinting, just as they used to, and his smile was as tantalising as ever.

Jane steeled herself against it. Lyall had always thought that all he had to do was smile and he would get his own way. It had worked before, but it wasn't going to work this time. 'I don't think so.'

'Why not?'

'We said all we had to say to each other ten years ago,' she said, looking determinedly away from his smile. 'I think it would be sensible to leave it at that.' And then she made the mistake of looking at him as he laughed.

'Jane,' he said. Only he had ever been able to say her name just that way, rippling with amusement and tender as a caress. 'Sensible Jane, you haven't changed at all!' Reaching across, he ran a careless finger down her cheek. 'But thank you for the lift.'

And then he was gone, the door banging behind him as he ran for the shelter of the pub, and Jane was left staring hopelessly at the rain, her heart awash with memories and her cheek still burning from his touch.

CHAPTER TWO

'AND if you're not ready to fix my hot water when I get home tonight, I shall personally ensure that you never work in this area again!' She swept to the end of her diatribe at last. 'You just be at the house at six o'clock, George, or I promise you that you'll regret it!'

Jane banged down the phone without waiting for a reply and glowered at the receiver. She was much too cross to let George Smiles start on his usual snivelling excuses.

It wasn't entirely his fault that she was in such a bad mood, Jane admitted to herself. Lyall's reappearance had left her on edge and restless. It wasn't *fair* of him to come back now. She was fine as she was, settled, stable, used to life without him. She didn't want him around, stirring up old feelings, old desires. She didn't want to remember how exciting everything had seemed when he was there, or to wonder again how things would have been if she hadn't seen him with Judith that day. She had buried the hurt and unhappiness deep inside her, hiding it behind the sensible practicality that she wore like a protective barrier, and told herself that she was grateful that she had found out the truth about Lyall before she had done anything stupid like leaving with him. No, Jane had learnt her lesson about love, and she had no intention of making the same mistake again.

But now Lyall was back, and she couldn't forget the careless brush of his fingers against her cheek.

The storm had rumbled on all night, and Jane had slept badly, waking to a damp, dreary morning. Nor had

her temper been improved by the non-appearance of
George Smiles that morning. She had got home from
visiting Miss Partridge yesterday evening to find that her
boiler had gone on the blink again, and that there was
no hot water. George was notoriously unreliable, but
after several fruitless phone calls in an attempt to track
down other plumbers Jane had been desperate, and he
had promised faithfully that he would be there to fix it
at eight o'clock that morning.

Jane had waited as long as she could before steeling
herself for a cold shower and driving into the office at
Starbridge with nothing to look forward to but a session
with the accounts and an interview with the bank
manager. It wasn't any wonder she was in a bad mood,
Jane decided, stabbing morosely at her calculator.

When Dorothy had buzzed to say that George was on
the phone, she had been more than ready to take her
temper out on him. The antiquated phones always cut
off the beginning of a sentence, but Jane was used to
that and as soon as she'd heard Dorothy say '-iles' she
had told her to put him through at once. Perhaps she
had been a bit hard on him. He had tried several times
to interrupt, but Jane had swept on, too glad of the
chance to tell George exactly what she thought of him
to listen to any of his feeble explanations.

Now her eyes fell on the clock, and she yelped as she
remembered her appointment with the bank manager.
Grabbing her handbag and jacket, she rushed out into
the front office where Dorothy, secretary and bastion of
Makepeace and Son, was typing out invoices.

'Well?' she asked with unaccustomed excitement.

'What?' If Jane had had time, she would have wondered at Dorothy's look of intense interest. She had told
her all about her frustration with George, of course, but
it normally took more than that to rouse Dorothy from
her placidity. As it was, Jane was wrestling with her um-

brella and trying to calculate how long it would take her
to find a park near the bank. 'Oh, it's OK,' she said in
a preoccupied voice. 'He's coming tonight.' Grimacing
at her watch and quite missing Dorothy's surprised expression, she headed for the door. 'I've got to run. See
you tomorrow, Dorothy.'

The meeting with the bank manager, Derek Owen, was
not a success. He was unconvinced by Jane's attempt to
sound confident about her chances of winning the
Penbury Manor contract, and unimpressed by her cerise
suit which she had worn specially in an attempt to look
like a successful businesswoman. When she emerged,
Jane felt thoroughly squashed, and her bad temper,
which had at least buoyed her up before, had crumbled
into a tired dreariness.

Dorothy only worked in the mornings, and had gone
by the time Jane got back to the office. She spent an
unprofitable afternoon trying to persuade herself that
the accounts weren't quite as depressing as they seemed
and pursuing a half-hearted argument with the timber
yard about their bill, but at ten to six she gave up and
drove the ten miles back to Penbury. The sun was struggling to break through the clouds, but the cow parsley
frothing along the sides of the roads was still damp and
drooping in sympathy with her spirits. The van hated
the wet too and spluttered alarmingly. The way things
were going today, it would probably choose this evening
to give up the ghost halfway back to Penbury, Jane
thought gloomily.

As if to disprove such a lack of confidence, a shaft
of sunlight burst through the clouds like a biblical picture
just as the van wheezed past the church at last and jerked
to an undignified halt outside the low stone house that
had been Jane's home for as long as she could remember.

She was in the middle of persuading herself that it was
a good omen when she realised that there was no sign

of George Smiles's van. Surely he hadn't let her down again, after all she had had to say to him this morning?

Scowling, she got out of the van and slammed the door shut behind her. 'George!' she called, in case he had left his van somewhere else for some obscure reason.

A figure moved in the porch and Jane blew out a breath in relief. So he *was* here! Just as well for him, she thought darkly, and headed for the gate, only to stop dead as Lyall Harding emerged and strolled confidently down the path towards her and her heart lurched to her throat.

'What are you doing here?' she demanded rudely to disguise her breathlessness. She was furious with herself. What was the point of spending the whole night convincing herself that Lyall's return wasn't going to affect her at all if her heart was going to behave like that every time she saw him?

Lyall opened the gate for her with a flourish, blue eyes dark and amused. 'I don't know why you're looking so surprised. You were the one who wanted to see me.'

'*I* wanted...?' Staggered at his effrontery, Jane glared at him. 'I most certainly did not!'

'Then why did you tell me to be here by six o'clock?'

Jane opened her mouth to deny telling him anything of the kind, and then closed it again as the awful truth dawned. 'You mean... it was you?' she said, not very coherently, but Lyall appeared to have no trouble understanding what she meant.

'It was,' he confirmed gravely, and although his expression was bland his eyes gleamed with humour. Jane remembered that look. It was the one he used to use when he was teasing her for being too staid, too sensible, too serious. She had learnt to laugh in the end, and he would grin and pull her into his arms and tell her that he loved her anyway.

She clamped down firmly on the memory. 'I thought you were George Smiles,' she said with an accusing look.

'So I gathered,' said Lyall drily.

It was just like him to let her make a fool of herself like that! 'You should have told me who you were,' said Jane in a severe voice.

'I did try,' he reminded her. 'But it would have taken a better man than me to stop you once you got started! I couldn't get a word in edgeways.'

'You could have done if you'd wanted to,' she said crossly, choosing not to remember how she had refused to listen to the voice's attempts to interrupt her. 'In fact,' she went on as she stalked past him up to the porch, 'I can't remember a time when you didn't do *exactly* as you wanted. Don't try and tell me you're not capable of interrupting anyone!'

'Not normally, perhaps,' Lyall admitted. 'But I was taken aback to hear you so cross. You always used to be so cool and moderate about everything. You would never have bawled out anyone the way you did this morning before.' He had kept up with her as she marched up the path and now glanced down at her with speculative blue eyes. 'You're a tougher lady than you used to be, aren't you?'

Jane kept her face bent over her bag as she searched for her key and thought of the years struggling to keep the firm going. 'I've had to learn to be,' she said with some bitterness. Lyall's betrayal had only been her first lesson.

Lyall lounged beside her, filling the porch with his presence, making her fingers fumble as she groped for the key. 'Are you tough inside too, Jane?' he asked. 'Or is it all just an act, just as that cool, capable air was always an act? You used to try so hard to be sensible, but inside you weren't sensible at all. You were warm and loving and much more vulnerable than you thought you were. You fooled everybody else, but you never fooled me.'

Jane refused to look at him. 'What are you doing here?' she said coldly as her fingers closed over the key at last.

'I've come to fix your boiler, of course.'

Her head jerked up in astonishment. 'You can't fix my boiler!'

'I might not be able to,' he agreed. 'I can't tell until I have a look at it.'

She looked at him, resentment at the easy way he could call up unwanted memories forgotten in her surprise. His jeans were faded but clean and the black sweatshirt he wore with the sleeves pushed up to his elbows, while absolutely plain, had an indefinably expensive look about it. 'You're a *plumber*?' Over the years she had imagined Lyall doing many things, but plumbing definitely wasn't one of them.

'Not really, no,' said Lyall casually. 'But I've done a few odd jobs in my time. Even if I can't fix it, I might be able to tell you what the problem is.'

She shouldn't have been so surprised. He had always been vague about work. Whenever Jane had asked him what he did, he would shrug and say, 'Anything.' He had turned up that summer with no sign of a job, apparently with plenty of money, but he had never said where it came from. He worked to earn enough to move on when he wanted to, was all he had told Jane when she'd persisted. He wasn't interested in a career or anything that tied him down. He wanted to be free.

It should have been a warning.

Now here he was again, apparently still surviving on odd jobs, thought Jane disapprovingly. 'You must be desperate for work,' she said with a suspicious look. Why else would he want to fix her boiler?

Lyall shrugged. 'Probably not as desperate as you are for hot water. Still, if you want to wait for George to turn up, I'll go...' Unconcerned, he turned as if to leave.

'No, wait!' Jane spoke before she thought. She had spent all day fantasising about being able to relax into a deep, hot bath and the prospect of another cold shower was too horrible to contemplate. She eyed Lyall with a sort of baffled resentment. How was it that he always managed to wrong-foot her? She wanted to tell him to go away and leave her alone almost as much as she wanted a hot bath—and Lyall knew it.

The dark blue eyes held amused understanding as he turned back to her. 'Well?' he said.

'Can you really mend my boiler?' she asked unwillingly.

'I can try. Why don't you let me take a look?'

'Well, since you're *here*...' Conscious of how ungracious she sounded, Lyall opened the door and stooped to pick up the post. It was impossible not to remember the last time Lyall had been in this house; her father's angry voice, the iciness around her heart, the look on Lyall's face as he'd turned and left.

Lyall gave no sign that he heard the echoes of the past as he followed Jane down the corridor to the kitchen. Crouching down by the boiler, he took off the cover to peer inside. Jane found herself watching his back and the way the jeans stretched over his powerful thighs, and her fingers tingled with an appalling urge to run her hand lightly down his spine and discover whether he still felt the same. She had loved the sleekness of his skin, and the steely strength of his body had been a refuge. Teasing her, taunting her, tempting her, Lyall had turned her life inside out, but when he'd held her in his arms nothing else had mattered.

Horrified at the train of her thoughts, Jane jerked her eyes away. 'W-would you like some tea?' she asked in a

high, tight voice. That was it: pretend he was just Chris
or Andrew or Kevin, or any of the other men who worked
for her and whose backs she never had the least desire
to touch.

'Thanks,' he said without looking round.

Jane's hand shook slightly as she held the kettle under
the gushing tap. She really must pull herself together.
The last thing she wanted was for Lyall to think that he
still had the power to affect her. He had surprised her,
that was all. First yesterday and now today, he had
caught her unawares, but it wouldn't happen again. Now
that she knew he was liable to turn up unexpectedly, she
would be on her guard. She would be just as cool and
collected as he had always accused her of being.

The thought reassured Jane, but it didn't quite stop
her eyes being drawn to where Lyall squatted by the
boiler. Picking up the post, she concentrated on the
letters instead while she waited for the kettle to boil.

At the bottom was a postcard from Kit. Jane turned
it over and read the message: Buenos Aires was a wonderful place and he was madly in love. Could she possibly
send him some more money as funds were getting low?

Typically Kit. Jane sighed and read it again. She had
already sent him as much as she could afford. Where
was she going to find any more?

'You look tired.' Lyall's abrupt voice broke into her
thoughts. Preoccupied by thoughts of Kit, Jane hadn't
noticed him straighten or turn, and he had been watching
her as she leant against the sink, frowning down at the
card. Her fine, honey-coloured hair was tucked behind
her ears, the businesslike suit was looking decidedly
creased and there were shadows under her grey eyes as
she looked up, startled.

'It's just been a long day, that's all,' she said, and
turned to make the tea, unnerved by the look of frowning
concern in those dark blue eyes. It had vanished anyway

by the time she had poured out a mug for him and handed it over, being very careful not to let her fingers touch his. 'Will you be able to fix the boiler?' she asked, keeping her voice deliberately cool and unconcerned.

'I think so. Have you got a screwdriver?'

'Of course.' She fetched her father's toolbox from under the stairs and set it on the kitchen table. Lyall raised his eyebrows as he surveyed the professional array of gleaming spanners and screwdrivers. Her father had always been meticulous about his tools.

'Quite a collection. I suppose they were your father's?'

'Yes,' said Jane shortly. She didn't want to talk to Lyall about her father.

'He would have liked a box like this, with everything neatly in its place,' he commented, selecting a screwdriver. 'Nice and orderly, like his life. If you didn't fit into the right slot, he didn't want to know, did he?'

'That's not fair!' she protested, stung by the grain of truth in the observation.

'Isn't it?' Lyall gave her an ironic look over his shoulder as he squatted back down by the boiler. 'He treated you just like one of these tools.'

'Rubbish!' said Jane furiously. 'Dad loved me!'

'Of course he did . . . but it didn't stop him wanting to keep you safely shut away where he knew where to find you. That's why he didn't like me. He was afraid I'd take you out and change you and then you wouldn't want to fit back into his organised scheme of things.'

Jane's lips tightened. 'You can't blame a father for wanting to protect his daughter.'

'I can if it stops the daughter having a life of her own,' said Lyall, squinting into the depths and inserting the screwdriver with care.

'Perhaps you'd think differently if you had a daughter,' snapped Jane. 'Or then, perhaps not. You'd probably let her do what she wanted as soon as she was out of nappies, just so that she didn't impinge on your precious freedom.'

'That's precisely why I don't intend to have any children,' he said coolly. 'I've never wanted the commitment of a wife and family. But if I did, I hope I'd be wise enough not to wrap them up in cotton wool the way your father did. They'd either end up totally repressed, like you, or go to the other extreme like your brother!'

Jane banged her mug down on the worktop. 'I am not repressed!'

Too late, she remembered saying exactly the same thing ten years ago. The past echoed in her ears, spilling out to swamp the kitchen with the warmth of that summer's day. They had been sitting by the stream, dangling their feet in the cool water. It was three days after that first mad trip to the sea. Just when Jane had decided that she had been no more than a temporary amusement to fill a dull day, Lyall had turned up on the doorstep and cajoled her into a picnic. Alarmed and intrigued by him, just as he had known she would be, Jane had resisted, then weakened, then succumbed.

'You're so uptight,' Lyall had said, his voice full of lazy amusement. Reaching out, he'd smoothed her hair behind her ear and she'd quivered at the brush of his fingers. 'Are you afraid of me, or are you just repressed?'

'I am not repressed!' Jane had sat up indignantly.

'Does that mean you're afraid of me?'

Her chin had gone up. 'Of course not!'

'Good,' he'd said, smiling in a way that had dissolved her bones. 'Then you won't mind if I kiss you, will you?'

And he had drawn her down into the sweet grass and Jane had been lost.

Awash with memories, Jane gazed despairingly at the back of Lyall's head. Oblivious to the distant reverberations of their first kiss, he grunted as the piece he had been unscrewing came free at last. Why did she have to remember when he so clearly didn't, or, if he did, couldn't care less?

'Why did you come here today?' she asked abruptly. 'You could have rung back and told Dorothy I'd mistaken you for someone else. And why were you ringing anyway?' she demanded, as the thought occurred to her for the first time. 'I wouldn't have thought you'd be interested in talking to anyone as *repressed* as I am,' she finished on a sarcastic note.

Lyall sat back on his heels and shrugged. 'I thought it was a pity we'd started off on the wrong foot yesterday,' he said. 'I realised I'd taken you by surprise, and I was going to apologise, that's all.'

'You didn't need to come round and fix the boiler instead,' Jane pointed out, unconvinced.

'I didn't have anything else to do,' he said, and then grinned. 'And it was pretty obvious that poor old George wouldn't dare to, at least not if he had any sense! Are you always that grumpy now?'

It wasn't fair of him to smile like that. Jane eyed him with resentment. 'You'd be cross if you'd had the day I've had,' she said waspishly. 'Normally, I can assure you that I'm not in the least "grumpy" as you call it.'

'You were pretty grumpy yesterday.'

Not until he had turned up. Jane's eyes slid away from his and she picked up her mug once more. 'I'm just fed up of waiting to hear whether bloody Multiplex or whatever it's called is going to give us the contract for Penbury Manor or not,' she muttered, swirling her tea morosely around the mug.

'So you haven't heard yet?' said Lyall, going back to the boiler.

'No, I haven't! None of us has! I rang the architect a couple of days ago and he said that *he* was waiting to hear as well. Apparently the company secretary can't make a decision until some fat-cat chairman stops playing golf and guzzling expensive lunches long enough to make up his mind.'

'Do you know anything about Multiplex?' he asked. His voice was quite neutral but it held an undercurrent of something that Jane couldn't quite identify.

'It's something to do with electronics,' she said vaguely, not entirely sure what electronics were.

'"Something to do with electronics?"' Lyall shook his head in disbelief. 'Multiplex is one of the largest electronics companies in Europe, Jane! Companies like that aren't run by chairmen who do nothing but play golf and go out to lunch.'

She hunched a shoulder. 'Well, why won't they make a decision about Penbury Manor, then?'

'It's just possible that they have other things to do,' he said sardonically. 'If I'd been in your position, Jane, I'd have made an effort to find out something about the company I was tendering to. If you'd bothered to do that, you'd have found out that Multiplex has a reputation for quality and efficiency, and that if they're not making a decision there's likely to be a good reason for it.'

'You seem to know a lot about it,' grumbled Jane as Lyall straightened.

'It's a very well-known company,' he said with an enigmatic look. 'As you'd know if you ever took an interest in anything outside Penbury!'

Jane opened her mouth to retort, then thought better of it. She wasn't going to get into *that* argument again! 'I'll be out in the garden if you need anything,' she said with freezing dignity, and stalked out.

The garden was damp and battered after the rain. Jane stooped over her pots, dead-heading geraniums savagely. How dared Lyall accuse her of being cross and unreasonable? He obviously thought she was an embit-

tered old spinster incapable of running a business
properly. What would *he* know about running a business,
anyway? The more she thought about his careless accusation about her bad temper, the crosser Jane got. She
wasn't cross. It was only Lyall who made her cross. She
wouldn't even have been cross with George if it hadn't
been for Lyall's turning up out of the blue like that and
throwing her off balance. Worry about the contract had
left her weary, but she had never taken it out on anyone
else before. Logically, she knew that she couldn't blame
Lyall for Multiplex's stalling, or the unreliability of her
boiler, or George's non-appearance, but Jane wasn't
feeling very logical. If he hadn't come back, she would
have dealt with problems as they arose in her usual calm,
capable way. As it was, she was jittery and jolted by the
unwelcome confrontation with the past, and incapable
of dealing with *anything*. And then Lyall wondered why
she was cross!

Still furiously tidying the geraniums, Jane discovered
to her dismay that she had snapped off a perfectly good
flower. That was Lyall's fault too!

'Sorry,' she apologised absurdly to the geranium.

'Why are you never as nice to people as you are to
plants, Jane?' Lyall's humorous voice came from the
doorway, and Jane straightened, flushing. Trust Lyall to
catch her talking to plants!

'Have you finished?' she asked more sharply than she
had intended.

'Yup. I'm just giving the tank a chance to heat up.'

'Oh.' Belatedly remembering that he was, in spite of
everything, doing her a favour, Jane wiped her dirty
hands on her suit without thinking, leaving a smear of
damp earth. 'Well—er—thank you,' she said awkwardly.

Lyall drank his tea, lounging casually against the door-
jamb and watching her over the rim of his mug with an
ironic expression. Jane always forgot how disconcert-

ingly acute his blue eyes could be when they weren't
gleaming with laughter, and she bent to brush the mud
off her skirt.

'Was that your boyfriend you were with in the pub
last night?'

The question caught Jane unawares and her heart
sank. Last night had not been a success. When Alan had
rung, she had seized on the chance to go out and take
her mind off Lyall, but to her dismay Alan had been
reluctant to go further than the village pub. After he had
driven out from Starbridge, Jane could hardly refuse to
go, and she had skulked into the bar behind him. For-
tunately Lyall had been in the other half of the pub, and
she hadn't thought he had noticed her. She had glimpsed
him across the bar when she'd gone to get a round, but
he had been engrossed in conversation with a glamorous
redhead and a blonde who kept shaking back her hair
and laughing just a little too loud. Smiling fixedly at
Alan, Jane had told herself that she was glad that Lyall's
attention was otherwise occupied.

Lyall drained his tea and set the mug on the low wall.
'Well?' he prompted.

'I fail to see that it's any of your business,' she said
coldly. 'But yes, that was Alan.'

'The man who makes you so extremely happy?'

Jane set her teeth. 'Yes.'

'You didn't look very happy,' said Lyall, as if considering the matter. 'I can't say I was surprised. He didn't
look your type.'

'I hate to point out the obvious, but you don't know
what my type is!'

'*I* used to be your type,' he reminded her softly.

Faint colour tinged Jane's fine cheekbones. 'That was
a long time ago,' she said curtly, turning away ostensibly
to check the undersides of the rose leaves for greenfly.
'I was young and silly then and didn't know any better,

but I've grown up in the last ten years. You look for quite different qualities in a man when you're twenty-nine than you do when you're nineteen.'

'Such as?'

'Such as kindness, reliability, security...none of which I associate with you!'

'Maybe I've grown up too,' Lyall suggested, and Jane glanced at him over her shoulder.

'You don't look as if you've changed very much to me.'

'Appearances can be deceiving,' he said blandly, adding unfairly, 'That was the first thing I discovered about you. So calm, so sensible...and so passionate underneath.'

The colour deepened in Jane's cheeks. 'I was going by experience, not by looks.'

'I see.' A faint smile touched the edges of Lyall's mouth. 'And is Alan Good as nice and safe as he looks?'

'Yes, he is,' she said defiantly. 'He's very nice.' He *was*, she encouraged herself. She always knew where she was with Alan. He never threw her off balance the way Lyall used to. She had never known *what* Lyall was going to do; there was a dangerously unpredictable quality about him that had alarmed and excited and enchanted her in turn. Alan might be duller, but he was much less exhausting to be with.

'Still a coward at heart,' mocked Lyall. 'You'd rather be safe and bored than take a chance on something more exciting.'

'Of course you *would* think that!' Jane swung round, eyes bright with indignation. 'Just because I wasn't stupid enough to go away with you!'

'Because you were stupid enough not to trust me,' he corrected her in a hard voice.

Unbidden, an image of him standing beneath the tree—their tree—with Judith in his arms wavered in front of Jane's eyes. 'Not trusting you was the only sensible thing I did that summer,' she said bleakly.

Cold and contemptuous, the blue eyes bored into hers, but Jane refused to quail before his look, and after a moment he turned back to the kitchen. 'I'll go and check the water,' he said tightly.

He was angry. Jane stared blindly at the geraniums and fought the memories of the day her world had shattered into tiny pieces. She had trusted Lyall, had put her heart in his hands, and he had betrayed her. She could still remember stumbling along the woodland path towards him, bursting into the clearing to see Judith held tightly in Lyall's arms... What right did *he* have to be angry?

'It's working now,' said Lyall in a carefully neutral voice, appearing once more, and Jane, turning to face him, was furious with herself for being relieved to see that the contempt had vanished from his eyes.

'Thank you,' she muttered.

'Look, it was all a long time ago,' he sighed after a moment. 'What's the point of arguing about something that happened ten years ago?'

He came to stand next to her by the low stone wall. He didn't touch her, but Jane was very conscious of his powerful body. Beneath her lashes, she could see his hands hooked into the pockets of his jeans and the fine dark hairs on his forearms. He had obviously washed his hands, but there was still a smear of oil on his strong wrist.

'It looks as if I'm going to be around for a while,' Lyall went on carefully when she didn't say anything. 'Why don't we just agree to put the past behind us and start again? It would be much easier if we pretended to be strangers, wouldn't it? We could just forget that we had ever been anything else.'

How could she forget? How could she forget the rocketing excitement of his kisses or the sleek, supple strength of his body beneath her hands?

And yet, wasn't Lyall right? If they were to treat each other as strangers, it might be easier to push the memories back where they belonged. She could behave normally once more, and he would see how mature and capable she really was.

'All right,' she said slowly. 'I'll try if you will.'

'That's agreed, then.'

'Yes.'

There was an awkward pause. At least, Jane felt awkward. Lyall looked just as he always did, utterly relaxed and assured, like a big cat lying in the sun. He had the same quality of leashed power, gave the same impression that at any instant the laziness and humour might vanish and something much more dangerous and unpredictable would spring into their place.

Lyall was watching her with an unreadable expression, and Jane shifted uncomfortably beneath his gaze. 'Well—er—how much do I owe you for fixing the boiler?'

He waved a dismissive hand. 'Forget it.'

'I thought we were supposed to be strangers?' she reminded him. 'I'd have paid one of the Makepeace and Son plumbers if one of them had come out, and George would have made me pay through the nose.'

'It's really not necessary,' he protested, but Jane had no intention of being beholden to him already.

'I'd rather pay you,' she said firmly. 'In fact, I insist on giving you something.'

A disquieting gleam of humour sprang to Lyall's eyes as he studied her face. 'Do you mean that?'

'Of course,' she said with dignity, pleased at the opportunity to show him just how capable she was of treating him like a stranger. 'Will you take a cheque?'

Lyall shook his head. 'I only accept payment in kind,' he said, and calmly reached out to take her by the shoulders. Instinctively, Jane tried to step back, but she was too late. His hands were already sliding up from her shoulders to cup her face between his palms and his thumbs drifted caressingly along her cheekbones. His touch was feather-light, but his hands held her as surely as if she were pinned against the wall.

'You really don't need to give me anything,' he murmured, looking down into Jane's eyes, which were wide and grey and bright with a confused mixture of alarm and longing. 'But since you insist...'

'No——' Jane began, but even as she lifted her hands to push him away his mouth came down on hers, and the ground dropped away beneath her feet as she spun giddily through ten years to the vividly remembered delight of his kiss. The electrifying touch of his lips; his hands, so warm, so sure; the inexpressible feel of his long, hard body...Jane was as helpless before them now as she had been before. Past arrowed into the piercing pleasure of the present, obliterating the pain and the hurt, shattering her resistance, leaving only the touch of him and the taste of him and the wonderful, glorious feel of him.

Without thinking, Jane melted against him, twining her arms around his neck as his hands drifted down her throat and lingered at her breasts before sliding round to gather her closer. This was what she had been thinking about ever since she had turned to see him standing on the path at Penbury Manor, ever since he had disappeared ten years ago. One look at his mouth had been enough to set the thought of his kiss burning deep inside her, and now the warm exploration of his lips was both a release and a possession, binding her back to him once more.

Murmuring her name, Lyall began kissing his way down her throat to follow the tantalising path of his hands, and Jane tangled her fingers in his hair, gasping at each intense shaft of remembered pleasure as his lips moved possessively over her skin. She clung to him, kissing his ear, his jaw, the pulse in his throat with a sort of desperation while her body arched towards his of its own accord and she sank unresisting beneath the tide of honeyed memories. A ragged sob did sound in her throat when Lyall brushed aside her jacket and began unbuttoning her blouse with unsteady fingers, but it was impossible to tell whether she was pleading or protesting. Her head was tipped back and she closed her eyes against the delirious whirl of sensation as his hands slid beneath the soft material, cupping and curving over her body, lifting her insistently to the searing, scorching touch of his mouth until she cried out.

Even the memories faded before this onslaught of passion. Jane was beyond thinking about the past or the future or why Lyall had come back, and the present meant only this intoxicating rush of sheer delight that left her molten in his arms. Their kisses grew deeper, hungrier, almost frenzied, and, almost frightened by them, she pushed her hands beneath his sweatshirt and dug her fingers into his back, clinging to the hard security of his body even as she gloried in the feel of compact strength and warm skin.

And then suddenly, inexplicably, it was over. Lyall was lifting his head, releasing her reluctantly. Jane clutched at him in protest as she felt him withdraw, but her arms fell away as he stepped back and drew her blouse together with hands that were hardly more steady than her own. For a long moment they just stared at each other, shocked by the passion that had swept them up like a tornado and vanished as abruptly as it had come. There was no laughter in the blue eyes now. Instead they held an unfathomable expression that Jane was in no state even to try and understand.

'That'll do nicely,' he said with a twisted smile, although his voice was quite steady. 'I think I'd better go before you decide that you've overpaid.'

Jane was incapable of saying anything. Without being aware of what she was doing of what she meant, she nodded dazedly, so disorientated by the abrupt return to reality that she could only clutch her blouse together and watch with huge, dark eyes as Lyall walked away and out through the kitchen to the front door.

CHAPTER THREE

'THANK heavens you've come!' Dorothy was bursting with news when Jane arrived at the office the next morning. 'I was beginning to wonder if something had happened to you.'

'I overslept,' said Jane, picking up the post and carefully avoiding Dorothy's sharp eyes. 'I didn't sleep very well last night.'

Boiling with rage and humiliation, she had lain awake long into the night, flaying herself with memories of the kiss that had left her shaken and appalled and horribly close to tears. She was furious with Lyall for kissing her like that, even more aghast at her own behaviour. What had possessed her to melt into his arms as if the last ten years had never happened? Jane had squirmed at the thought. He had hurt her and used her and betrayed her, but when he kissed her all she could do was kiss him back as if she was just as much in love with him as she had been before!

Well, she wasn't! Jane had punched her pillow into shape and thrown herself over on to her back once more. She had got over Lyall a long time ago, and if he thought one kiss was going to change anything he had another think coming! Of course, it was typical of him to catch her off guard with all that talk of putting the past behind them. She should have known better than to trust him, she'd thought bitterly. Lyall wouldn't be happy until he had smashed the safe, secure world that she had reconstructed so carefully around her, but she wasn't going to give him the opportunity. Her best defence lay in being the cool, sensible girl she had tried so hard to be over the last ten years, the girl she had been before he'd turned her life upside-down before. The next time they met— if they met again—she would be prepared, she'd vowed to herself. She would be crisp, unruffled, unconcerned, and with any luck Lyall would begin to wonder whether he had imagined that kiss after all.

The dawn light had been filtering through the curtains before Jane had fallen at last into an exhausted sleep so deep that she had slept right through her alarm. Now she stood by Dorothy's desk and looked through the post, and wished she felt as confident as she had in the early hours of the morning. Her body was still strumming with the memory of Lyall's mouth and Lyall's hands, and, no matter how hard she stared down at the letters, all she could see was the devilry dancing in his eyes as he had bent his head towards hers...

'I know you wanted to hear the news yourself,' Dorothy was saying apologetically, and Jane looked up from the post at last.

'What news?'

Dorothy stared. 'The news about Penbury Manor. Michael White rang about half an hour ago. Apparently Multiplex has come to a decision at last.'

In her preoccupation with Lyall's kiss, Jane had completely forgotten about the manor contract. 'And?' she said, suddenly alert.

'And we've got the contract!'

It was just the news Jane had needed. In her heart she had almost given up hope of being able to keep Makepeace and Son going any longer, and she had been dreading telling Dorothy and the men that there was no more work for them. Now the relief was so great that Jane felt almost giddy with it. It was only now that she had been thrown the lifeline of the manor contract that she really appreciated just how close to disaster the firm

had come, and the experience was a salutary reminder
of her priorities. She had been blowing that wretched
kiss out of all proportion. Her father had trusted her to
carry on the firm, and that was what was mattered most,
that and the people who worked for her and looked to
her for a living. Makepeace and Son was her life now,
and Lyall had no place in it.

After the long, frustrating weeks of waiting for a decision, there was suddenly a lot to do. Multiplex apparently wanted an initial meeting with the architect and all
the contractors that very day, so Jane had to be at the
manor at two o'clock, but before she went she called all
the men into the office and told them the news herself.
There had been many times over the last few years when
Jane had longed to stop struggling with accounts and
contracts and unreliable suppliers and go back to horticulture, but today the look on the men's faces made it
all worthwhile.

'Your dad would be proud of you,' Ray told her on
behalf of them all, and the warmth of the echoing cheer
brought a sudden sting of tears to Jane's eyes.

Buoyed up by their support, she drove up to the manor
in an optimistic mood. It would be too much to say that
she had forgotten Lyall, but she was doing her best to
push him firmly to the back of her mind and concentrate instead on being a crisply efficient contractor.

Some of that crispness wilted as she parked outside
the manor, the van looking old and shabby next to the
array of sleekly high-powered cars ranged on the gravel.
They were a sign of the changes to come, and Jane
thought with a pang of how the old house was going to
be transformed into yet another soulless business enter-
prise, but then caught herself up sternly. If Makepeace
and Son didn't do the work, then someone else would,
and jobs for the men who worked for her surely meant
more than worn flagstones and quirky fireplaces and

generations of children for whom this old house had been a home.

Straightening her spine, Jane tucked her clipboard under her arm and headed for the front door. Inside, she found everyone congregated in the panelled dining-room. Miss Partridge had sold most of the larger pieces of furniture with the house, and the vast refectory table was set with a number of high-backed oak chairs. She had spoken on the phone to Dennis Lang, who was company secretary at Multiplex, but most of her dealings so far had been with the architect, Michael White, and it was Michael who introduced her around. Multiplex had evidently decided to use local contractors wherever possible, for she recognised almost everyone, except for the Multiplex executives and Dimity Price, who was apparently going to be responsible for the interior design.

Dimity was frothy and feminine, with a tumble of Pre-Raphaelite blonde curls, wide green eyes and a breathy, little-girl voice. Next to her Jane felt inhibited and austere in fawn trousers and a crisp white shirt, but she smiled briefly and shook Dimity's hand, mentally raising her eyes. *Dimity*? The accent was definitely on the 'Dim', she decided before remembering that that was precisely the kind of comment that had led to Lyall's accusing her of being cool and repressed. He would certainly never accuse Dimity of being repressed: she was the kind of girl who overflowed with emotion.

Annoyed with herself for letting Lyall intrude on her thoughts, Jane turned away, to find Dennis Lang at her elbow. 'We're just waiting for the chairman,' he said, courteously handing her a cup of coffee. 'He's just been called away to take a transatlantic phone call, but he shouldn't be long, and we can get started as soon as he gets back.'

'I didn't realise the chairman would be here,' said Jane in surprise. 'Chairmen don't usually bother with this kind of detail, do they?'

'This chairman does,' Dennis said with a look of humorous resignation. 'He bothers with *every* detail. It's one of the secrets of his success, and this restoration project is one of his particular interests. He wants to be involved in every stage.'

Jane's heart sank. There was nothing worse than clients who wanted to be involved.

'It'll be wonderful to work with someone so *committed*,' gushed Dimity, who had floated over in time to catch the end of their conversation. 'And he's such a *charming* man—you'll adore him, Jane!'

Jane looked at Dennis. 'Will I?' she asked drily, and his eyes twinkled.

'He's usually very popular with the ladies,' he conceded, and nodded over her shoulder. 'But you must judge for yourself... here he is now.'

Two men had just come into the room, but Jane didn't need to be told which one was the chairman. Relaxed and self-assured in an immaculate grey suit, he exuded an indefinable but instantly identifiable air of power that made him the effortless focus of all attention. It was clear just by looking at him that here was a man who held his huge company under tight control, a man used to taking risks and winning.

A man she knew only too well.

It was Lyall.

Jane felt sick. She stared across the room at him, aghast, while her own scornful words seemed to echo around the room. 'You shouldn't be here... Some ghastly high-tech company is going to ruin it... Some fat-cat chairman... playing golf and guzzling expensive lunches...'

The words bounced back at her off the oak panelling and rang in her ears. A great, rushing, rolling wave of shock and humiliation engulfed her, so that although she stood rooted to the spot she felt as if she was floundering, tumbling breathlessly over and over and unable to find her feet.

Across the room, Lyall's dark head was bent courteously to listen to something Michael White was saying to him, but as Jane stared in horrified realisation he glanced over towards her. Mocking blue eyes looked straight into appalled grey ones, and he smiled unmistakably.

How he must be enjoying this moment! Michael was bringing him across to introduce him to her, and Jane felt the first wave of shock ebbing into a slowly gathering swell of sheer rage. How dared he make such a fool of her? He could easily have told her who he was, could at least have warned her instead of letting her face him in front of all these people quite unprepared, but no! That wouldn't have amused him nearly as much, would it?

Lyall let Michael make the introductions as if he had never met Jane before in his life. 'How do you do?' he said gravely, but the dark blue eyes were alight with amusement as he held out his hand.

With Michael's eyes on her, Jane had little choice but to take it, but it was a mistake. The feel of his fingers closing around hers brought back the memory of yesterday's kiss in a terrifying rush. Only a matter of hours ago, she had been gasping beneath the touch of his lips and the hungry exploration of his hands, and now he was calmly standing there, looking cool and dark and *devilish* while her world fell apart all over again.

Muttering something, she snatched her hand away. They all took their places around the table but Jane hardly heard a word of the introduction. She sat as far

away from Lyall as possible, but she was aware only of
him, of the heart-clenching line of his mouth and the
strong hands resting so confidently on the back of his
chair as he stood and talked. She had never seen him in
a suit before, she realised. It made him look older, more
dangerous, and ruthlessly competent. Why hadn't she
seen that before?

What an *idiot* she had been! Why hadn't she thought
about how he had changed? Why hadn't she guessed
when he'd turned up at Penbury Manor that he was
something to do with Multiplex? He had practically *told*
her in the kitchen, but had she put two and two together?
Of course she hadn't! Jane was furious with herself, even
angrier with Lyall for so patently enjoying her dis-
comfiture. Her earlier resolve to pretend that nothing
had happened rang hollow now. How could she ignore
him when he turned out to be Makepeace and Son's
major client?

Lyall was talking about his plans for the manor and
handing round sketches, and everyone was oohing and
aahing admiringly. 'It all looks *marvellous*,' sighed
Dimity, who, unlike Jane, had chosen to sit as close to
Lyall as possible. When the sketches reached her, Jane
barely glanced at them before passing them on. She was
simmering with suppressed rage. It had been so wonderful to get the news of the contract this morning and
feel that everything was going to work out after all, and
now it was all spoilt, and it was all Lyall's fault. It was
his fault for coming back, for kissing her, for standing
there so cool and assured while all she wanted to do was
hit him!

Suddenly she realised that everyone was looking at
her in expectant silence, and her gaze focused sharply
on the mockery in Lyall's dark blue eyes as he watched
her with one eyebrow raised enquiringly. She hadn't

heard a word he had said, and it was obvious that he knew it.

'I'm sorry?' she said tightly, wrenching her mind back to the meeting.

'I was just asking whether you had enough men available to start work straight away,' Lyall said with humiliating patience.

Jane set her teeth. 'Of course.'

'Good.' His face was still perfectly straight, but Jane didn't need to look into those glinting eyes to know that he was laughing at her. 'There's a rumour going round that I spend my whole time on the golf course or tucking into expense account lunches,' Lyall went on with deliberate provocation. 'I'm here to assure you all that that is not the case. I like to know exactly what's going on, and I intend to be down here often to check on progress. You will have noticed from the plans that the upper floor of the west wing has been designed as a self-contained flat. I'd like Makepeace and Son to start work by making it habitable, so that I can stay here when I come down.' He looked at Jane. 'I presume you've no objection to a temporary intensive effort before the specialised work begins?'

'Would it matter if I had?' said Jane, meeting his gaze angrily. The others looked aghast at her hostile tone, but she didn't even notice. Their eyes locked across the length of the table, it was as if she and Lyall were alone in the room.

'Does that mean you do object?' he said, and although his voice was insultingly even there was no mistaking its undercurrent of steel.

'I'm in no position to object, as you're well aware,' she snapped, beyond caring what he or anyone else thought. 'My only concern is for my men, and frankly I'd have thought you'd be better off spending your time overseeing your own company than checking up on mine.

They're all highly skilled craftsmen, and they can't work properly with the client hanging over them, quibbling and criticising and changing his mind just when they're halfway through a job.'

'I won't change my mind,' said Lyall. The glinting laughter had vanished from his eyes, leaving them an implacable blue. 'I decide what I want, and I make sure I get it.' Yes, he had always done that, Jane remembered bitterly. 'I've got no intention of interfering with your men,' he went on, the steel very pronounced now, 'but surely you'll agree that I'm entitled to take an interest in what they're doing? If I've got any comments, I'm quite prepared to liaise with you. After all,' he added deliberately, 'that's what you're there for, isn't it?'

'I object to having my time wasted unnecessarily,' said Jane, ignoring Michael's anguished signals for her to be quiet. 'If you don't think Makepeace and Son can do the job without you hanging over them, you'd better find yourself another building contractor!' Her chair scraped over the stone flags as she pushed back her chair, her grey eyes bright with antagonism. 'Perhaps you'd let me know when you've decided,' she said to Lyall. 'Either you trust our reputation and let us get on with the job, or you find a contractor whose men don't mind being hassled every five minutes!'

There was utter silence as she marched out of the room without looking back, head held high. Still borne on a wave of fury and humiliation, she stalked across the gravel to her van and reversed out, tyres squealing in protest, swinging the wheel round to face the drive. She made it back to the office in record time and screeched into the yard, slamming on the brakes just in time to avoid crashing into a pile of timber that had appeared since she had left. The suppliers had been quick off the mark once news of the contract had got round.

Jane switched off the engine. In the sudden silence, she looked from the timber to the familiar sign stretching above the office door. 'Makepeace and Son' was picked out in gold on a dark green background. For as long as Jane could remember, for as long as her father had been able to remember, that sign had been there, repainted in fresh green and gold every few years.

'What have I done?' Jane said out loud as the hot rush of anger evaporated into a hollow sense of disaster. She thought of the men who had toasted her so cheerfully that lunchtime, of the suppliers who must have been waiting by the phone for news of the contract on which so many jobs depended. How was she going to tell them that she had thrown the contract back in Lyall Harding's face?

Overwhelmed by horror at her own foolishness, Jane closed her eyes and dropped her forehead on to her hands, which were still gripping the top of the steering-wheel. 'What have I done?' she whispered despairingly again.

She squeezed her eyes tighter, but it was impossible to shut out the image of Lyall standing at the end of the table and watching her with hard blue eyes as she walked out. She knew quite well what she had done: she had jeopardised the future that had begun to look so much brighter for all of them, just because of Lyall and the way he made her feel.

Jane opened her eyes to stare at the sign once more. What was it Ray had said? 'Your dad would be proud of you.' Her face twisted. Her father would have been far from proud. He had spent his life building up Makepeace and Son into a thriving business, and he would have been bitterly ashamed if he could have seen the way she had just thrown it all away. He had never let his men down the way she had just done, and now it was up to her to do what she could to put things right.

And there was only one thing she *could* do.

Jane switched on the engine again, reversed out of the yard and drove slowly back to Penbury Manor.

The meeting had obviously broken up shortly after she had left, for most of the cars had gone. Reluctant to face anyone just yet, Jane parked the van in the shade, where it was half hidden by the drooping branches of a copper beech, and sat for a while, staring at the front door as she tried to get up her courage.

As she looked, it opened, and Dimity came tripping down the steps. She was patting her curls and looking very pleased with herself. Jane's eyes narrowed. It would be ages before they were in a position to start decorating. Why had Dimity found it necessary to stay on? It was a bit early to discuss wallpaper designs ... or had they found something much more interesting to discuss?

Jane watched bleakly as Dimity got into her car and twisted the rear-view mirror round to check her reflection. She delicately touched the edges of her eyes and then, apparently satisfied that her appearance had been as softly feminine as she desired, she put the car into gear and drove away without even noticing Jane's van beneath the tree.

Jane bit her lip. She rarely bothered about her own appearance, but now, on an impulse, she twisted her mirror round as Dimity had done to study her reflection. Her face looked gaunt and white and her eyes were dark with guilt. She could hardly have been more of a contrast to Dimity's pretty helplessness. There had never been anything helpless about Jane—until Lyall had kissed her.

She mustn't start thinking about Lyall kissing her, Jane reminded herself desperately as she got out of the van and wiped her damp palms on her trousers. She must think about the contract and the men who were depending on her to keep their jobs. Taking a deep breath, she walked across the gravel to the front door.

It was opened by the secretary who had been taking notes during the meeting. Her eyes widened as she saw Jane standing there with her hands clutched tightly together.

'I'd like to see Mr Harding, please.'

Lyall was standing by the bay window in the old library, talking to Dennis Lang, but he broke off abruptly as the secretary opened the door and announced Jane in apologetic tones.

'Dennis, would you mind leaving us?' he said, and waited until the older man had closed the door behind him before walking over to where Jane stood looking rigid and strangely vulnerable by the door, her grey eyes huge in her fine-boned face.

'Well?' he said in a hard voice.

Jane swallowed. 'I came back to apologise. I shouldn't have walked out of the meeting like that.'

'No, you shouldn't.' When she risked a look at his face, his eyes were cold and uncompromising. 'You made me look a fool.'

Her jaw dropped. 'I made *you* look a fool?' she echoed incredulously.

'I'm not used to being harangued at meetings,' said Lyall in a stinging voice. 'Nor to appointing contractors who walk out on me. You made it look as if my judgement was seriously at fault.'

'I'm sorry,' she muttered.

Lyall turned away with an exclamation of impatience and strode over to the window. 'I thought you wanted this contract?' he said abruptly over his shoulder. The letter you sent when you submitted your tender certainly made it sound as if you were desperate for the work!'

'I was.' Jane was more intimidated than she cared to admit by this new, stern Lyall, but she gritted her teeth and stood her ground. 'I am.'

'You've got a funny way of showing it,' he pointed out, still grim-faced. 'If the contract means so much, why throw it away like that?'

'You know why,' she said resentfully, and he swung round to regard her once more, hands thrust into his trouser pockets.

'Suppose you tell me anyway?'

The dark blue eyes were cool and faintly contemptuous, and Jane, who would have liked to meet them bravely, let her gaze slide away. Folding her arms defensively around her, she walked edgily over to the bookshelves and stared unseeingly at the worn leather spines.

'Why didn't you tell me who you were?' she burst out at last.

Lyall was still watching her from the other side of the room. 'You know who I am, Jane,' he said coolly. 'Few people know better.'

'You know what I mean! You could have told me that you were chairman of Multiplex!'

'And you could have found out for yourself,' he retorted. 'If you were half as sensible as you claim to be, you'd have made it your business to find out exactly who your client was, so don't blame me for your lack of professionalism. If you'd done your research, you'd have been prepared to see me here today.'

'Was I supposed to be prepared for you to turn up on my doorstep pretending to be a plumber, too?'

'I didn't pretend to be a plumber,' Lyall corrected her inexorably. 'All I said was that I'd done a number of different jobs in my time, which is true.'

'And your current job as chairman of a huge electronics company and owner of Penbury Manor just happened to slip your mind, is that it?'

He ignored her sarcasm. 'No, but unlike you I'm capable of keeping my private and professional life quite separate, and frankly I didn't think you'd believe me even if I told you. You always were prepared to think the worst of me, weren't you?'

'It's not what you think, Jane.' Lyall had caught up with her before she was out of the woods.

'Leave me alone!' Jane was crying, dashing the tears furiously from her cheeks.

'No, not until you listen to me.' He caught hold of her arm, but she jerked it away.

'I've listened enough to you,' she cried. Her face was blotched and her breath coming in great, gulping sobs. 'I should have listened to my father instead. He told me not to get involved with you. Everyone knew what you were like, but I was too stupid to listen!'

Lyall's face had closed. '*You* know what I'm like, Jane. Or haven't the last few weeks meant anything?'

'Not to you, apparently!' Jane swung round, distraught. 'I thought you were in love with me, and all the time you've been carrying on with that little tramp behind my back!'

'Don't you dare talk about Judith like that!' His voice was like a whiplash and Jane took an involuntary step backwards. 'She's not like that, and I haven't been "carrying on", as you put it, with her or anyone else.'

'Do you really expect me to believe that?' That scene under the tree was burnt into Jane's mind, Judith in Lyall's arms, her red head so close to his dark one. She could hardly believe that he had the nerve to stand there and deny it.

'Yes, I do,' he said coldly. 'I expect you to trust me—or would you rather trust all those nasty, mean-minded gossips who've had it in for me from the start?'

'I know what I saw,' said Jane stubbornly, resenting him even more for making her feel as if she was the one in the wrong.

'No, Jane, you don't know what you saw. All you know is what you choose to believe, and that makes you as petty and prejudiced and small-minded as everyone else round here!' Lyall gave an exclamation of disgust. 'I thought you were brave enough to think for yourself, but you aren't, are you? You don't want to be different. You're too much of a coward for that. You want to stay in your nice, safe little rut and let everyone else do your thinking for you. Well, if that's what you want, you stay there, but don't expect me to hang around waiting for you!'

Now they faced each other again, and in the old library the past jangled between them while the silence stretched unbearably. It was Lyall who broke it, sitting down behind the desk and studying Jane, who still stood stiffly by the bookshelves. Her fine, silky hair was tucked behind her ears and her chin was tilted at a proud angle. Silhouetted against the dark books in her white shirt and fawn trousers, she looked crisp and slender and much more vulnerable than she realised. Lyall sighed.

'For a sensible girl, Jane, you've behaved very stupidly! God knows how you've managed to keep the firm going as long as you have. Do you behave like this with all your clients?'

Jane was down, but still fighting. She lifted her chin even higher and met his eyes squarely. 'Do you behave like this with all your contractors?'

A gleam of appreciation lit the unsettling blue eyes. 'I'm not the one who walked out of the meeting,' he reminded her.

'And I didn't kiss you last night,' she snapped before she had time to think what she was saying.

'Didn't you, Jane?' said Lyall softly, the glinting amusement suddenly very pronounced. 'I thought you did.'

Jane struggled to stay cool, but she could feel the treacherous colour creeping up her throat and staining her cheeks. 'You know what I mean,' she said stiffly. 'You knew perfectly well that you would see me here today. I don't think that suggesting that we behave as strangers and then kissing me just before we had to discuss a major contract really puts you in a position to lecture me about professional behaviour!'

The stern line of Lyall's mouth had relaxed. 'No, well, it was an irresistible impulse...and it's not as if I'd never kissed you before.'

'That's not the point!'

'No,' he agreed unexpectedly. 'The point is whether you want this job or not, isn't it, Jane?'

She drew a deep breath. 'Yes.'

Lyall got restlessly to his feet. 'We had several more competitive tenders from other firms for this contract,' he told her, prowling over to the window. 'I chose Makepeace and Son because of its reputation for quality.'

'Then it wasn't because——' Jane began involuntarily, then broke off.

He lifted an eyebrow. 'Because what?'

'Because we'd...known each other before?'

'No. I've told you before, Jane, I keep my personal life quite separate from business. It was Dennis's job to study all the tenders and make recommendations, and because he knows how I feel about quality Makepeace and Son was top of his list. I recognised the name, of course, so I asked Dennis to find out more. I thought I might have to deal with your father, but Dennis said that you were running the firm on your own. Apparently you've made quite a reputation for yourself locally. Dennis told me you were supposed to be cool, unflappable and utterly reliable—although no one seeing how you behaved at that meeting today would believe it!'

'I'm not often confronted with ex-lovers without warning,' said Jane tartly before she could help herself, then caught herself up. She had come here to beg, and she had better get on with it. 'Look, I know I behaved very badly. I wasn't expecting to see you and after last night... well, I wasn't prepared. Normally I am just as coolly professional as they say.' She hesitated, but Lyall didn't help her by saying anything, and she forced herself to look directly into his eyes. 'You've got every right to give the contract elsewhere,' she went on doggedly. 'But I'd be very grateful if you would at least consider giving Makepeace and Son another chance.'

Lyall didn't answer immediately. He was watching the pride struggling with the humiliation in her face, and his eyes held a curious expression as he considered. Jane held her breath. Her whole future depended on what Lyall said now.

'On two conditions,' he said at last, and Jane was so relieved that she would have agreed to anything.

'What are they?'

'First, that there's no repetition of your behaviour this morning,' said Lyall astringently. 'I expect the people I work with to act in a professional way at all times, and if you're not prepared to be businesslike about the job, then I will have no compunction about offering the second and third stages of the contract to someone else.'

'That won't be necessary,' said Jane, flushing. She had asked for it, after all. She set her teeth and steeled herself for the rest of it. 'What's the second condition?'

Lyall looked down into her apprehensive grey eyes, his own expression inscrutable. 'That you have dinner with me tonight.'

CHAPTER FOUR

JANE stared at him. Whatever she had been expecting, it hadn't been that! 'You're not serious?'

'Why not?' he countered.

'It seems an odd sort of condition for someone supposedly so keen on being professional,' she said, unable to keep the waspish edge from her voice. 'I thought you believed in keeping your personal life and your business life quite separate?'

The disconcertingly enigmatic expression in Lyall's eyes dissolved into an amusement that managed to be both familiar and even more disconcerting. 'What could be more businesslike than dinner with my new contractor?' he asked.

Jane eyed him suspiciously. 'Will you be taking all your other contractors out to dinner?'

'Undoubtedly, but since none of them can start work until you've finished it seems reasonable to start with you.'

'Oh.' Jane's expression was uncertain. The last thing she wanted was to have dinner with Lyall, but she wasn't sure that she liked being relegated to a mere business contact either. Why was it that Lyall always managed to catch her off balance? One minute he was grimly formidable, the next inviting her out to dinner, though in such a way that made it impossible to know what his motives were. Experience had taught her to be chary of Lyall when he was at his most innocuous, and, unsure of how to react, Jane sought refuge in belligerence. 'Are the other contractors going to have dinner written in as part of their contract?'

'None of them has made the mistake of throwing their contracts back in my face,' Lyall reminded her with a sort of steely smoothness. 'You, however, are more in need of some urgent PR, so if you want to retain the contract I would strongly advise you to accept nicely.'

'That's blackmail!' Jane protested indignantly.

Lyall was unmoved by the accusation. 'It's good business,' he said. 'You've already jeopardised the contract once, Jane. If you had any business sense at all, you would have invited *me* to dinner.'

'Why on earth should I want to do that?'

'I'd have thought it was obvious,' he said, lifting his brows in faint surprise. 'If I'd done everything I could to antagonise a major client whose decision affected the future of my company, I'd be doing my damnedest to keep him sweet. What I *wouldn't* do is treat a simple invitation to dinner as if he was trying to wheedle me into white slavery!'

'You might if you knew as much about him as I know about you,' said Jane crossly, quite forgetting her earlier resolve to grovel.

For a moment she thought she had gone too far. His mouth hardened, and the expression in the blue eyes made her heart falter, but the next instant it had dissolved into a reluctant, exasperated smile as he shook his head.

'You've got nerve, Jane, I'll give you that! I can't think of anyone else who would risk losing a contract twice in one day, just for the sake of dinner! I'm beginning to wonder whether you really want this contract after all.'

'I do,' said Jane hastily, recognising the threat implicit in his words, and too harassed to pick her own with care. 'I mean, if it matters so much, of course I'll have dinner with you.'

'I've had more gracious responses to a dinner invitation,' said Lyall, but Jane saw with some relief that the corner of his mouth had curled up as if he was trying not to show that he was amused. 'I hope you're going to be nicer tonight?'

'Is being nice going to be written into the contract as well?' she asked sharply.

The blue eyes glinted down at her. 'Do you think it should be?'

'No,' said Jane quickly before she could get herself into any deeper water. 'Since this is going to be a purely business dinner, I'm sure we'll be able to be pleasant to each other.'

'I should hope so,' said Lyall with a mocking look. 'Think of it as a way of giving me some of that personal attention you promised me in your letter.' He turned away to open the door. 'I'll pick you up at half-past seven.'

It was clearly the end of the interview. Having got his own way, as usual, Lyall reverted to being a brisk executive. Jane didn't know whether to be relieved or put out at the pointed way he held open the door for her. 'Wear something smart,' was all he said as she walked past him, and before she had a chance to swallow her pride and thank him for letting her keep the contract he had shut the door on her and she was left with the obscure, sinking feeling that he had got the better of her yet again.

Still, at least she could face Dorothy knowing that they had the contract again. A dinner with Lyall wasn't too high a price to pay for that, surely? All she had to do was pretend that he was a mere business acquaintance. A meal, a glass of wine, a cool goodnight; what could be so hard about that? Nothing—if it were anyone other than Lyall. Jane parked the van outside the office and reflected glumly that he was the one person she could never treat in the cool, collected way she treated everyone else. Her reputation was well-founded. After her disastrous affair with Lyall, she had been determined never to let herself be hurt like that again, and she had buried her vulnerability deep, retreating behind an armour of crisp competence that effectively kept others at arm's length. The warm, vibrant girl that Lyall had teased into life all those summers ago had been an aberration, one that she had been careful to deny ever since. Her family and friends had been relieved to see the old sensible Jane reappear, and over the years she had convinced herself that that was the real Jane. Only now Lyall was back, and the protective layers of calmness and practicality had cracked at his first smile. Jane felt as if she was walking on ice, her heart in her mouth, knowing that one unwary movement would send her world tumbling once more. Dinner with Lyall was the last thing she needed as she struggled to keep her balance.

It took ages to decide what to wear that night. Jane tried on almost everything in her wardrobe before she settled on a white sleeveless shirt with an embroidered collar and a soft skirt in that warm shade somewhere between pink and red. Cinching a wide suede belt around her waist, she twisted in front of the mirror and wriggled her feet into low pumps. She didn't want to provoke Lyall unnecessarily by not following his instructions to look smart, but nor did she want it to look as if she had made any great effort for him.

Jane was stupidly nervous as she waited for him to arrive. It was another lovely summer evening, but she was blind to the golden light and the drifting scent of jasmine. She prowled edgily around the back garden, trying to convince herself that Lyall was just another client, but when the bell rang she knew that she had been wasting her time. No other client made her heart spin in sickening anticipation or sent her blood thundering through her veins until she could hardly hear herself think.

She took a deep, steadying breath. She was sensible Jane Makepeace and she was not—absolutely, definitely *not*—going to let Lyall provoke her or unsettle her or make her forget just how cool and businesslike she really was. Smoothing her hands on her skirt, she composed her face into an expression of polite indifference and opened the door.

Lyall was standing easily there, one hand raised to ring the bell again, but he lowered it when he saw Jane. In dinner-jacket and bow-tie, he looked darkly, dangerously attractive, and she had the strangest sensation that she had never seen him properly before. Everything about him was suddenly sharply distinct: the creases around his eyes, the cool planes of his face, the hard, exciting line of his mouth. Jane felt the breath leak slowly out of her. Lyall too looked oddly taken aback at the sight of her and for a long, long moment they just stared at each other as if this meeting were quite unexpected instead of negotiated only hours before.

Predictably it was Lyall who recovered first. 'Hello, Jane,' he said.

Only he had ever been able to say her name like that. 'Jane'. It was such a simple sound but Lyall made it vibrate with warmth and promise.

'Hello,' she said weakly, reflecting that it would be so much easier to show him just how cool and businesslike she was if only she could get her lungs to work properly.

'Are you ready?'

'Yes.' Appalled at how husky her voice sounded, Jane cleared her throat. Cool, businesslike...remember? 'I'll just get my bag.'

Lyall watched her as she locked the door and put the keys away in her bag. Her head was bent as she fumbled with the zip pocket with unsteady fingers, and her shiny brown hair slithered forward to hide her face. Glancing up without warning, she caught such a curious expression in his blue eyes that she stopped uncertainly.

'Is something the matter?'

'No.' She had the feeling that he was as disconcerted as she was. 'I was just...surprised.'

'Surprised?'

'Perhaps I expected that you would have changed your mind,' he said.

'I can't think why,' said Jane, unaccountably ruffled. 'You made it very clear what would happen if I did...but then you always did get exactly what you wanted, didn't you?'

'Not always,' said Lyall softly and, reaching out without haste, he smoothed a stray brown hair behind Jane's ear. His fingers grazed against her skin like fire and her heart contracted with memories as she stepped breathlessly back.

'Shall we go?'

The car waiting by the gate was sleek and expensive, with deep, luxurious leather seats. Lyall held the door open for her, and Jane was careful not to brush against him as she got in. She was still strumming from that brief, casual touch and the odd look in his eyes. This was a business dinner, she told herself desperately, and Lyall was just a client, a mere acquaintance, almost a stranger.

It was a long, still summer evening. Jane could smell the lush grass along the hedgerows brushing against the car as it purred through the slanting shadows, and the golden light fell warm on her cheek through the open sunroof. The rippling notes of a piano concerto filled the car. Lyall drove well, not in the reckless, neck-or-nothing way he used to, but with his hands very steady on the wheel. They kept catching at the edge of Jane's vision. No matter how hard she tried to look at the passing countryside, her gaze would flicker towards his profile, glancing along the line of his cheek and jaw to settle on the corner of his mouth, and the breath would dry in her throat before she managed to wrench her eyes away again.

Determined to prove to him once and for all that she was a cool, composed woman of twenty-nine and not the impressionable teenager whose bones had once dissolved at his merest touch, Jane kept up a flow of brittle conversation that acquired an increasingly desperate edge the further they drove. Lyall replied gravely with equal politeness, but his voice was edged with amusement, as if he was indulging her in some game, and Jane felt her composure fray.

It was a relief when the car slowed and turned off the road, but her carefully cool image slipped altogether when Lyall drew up outside one of the most famous restaurants in the country.

'We're not going in *here*?'

Lyall quirked an eyebrow at her as he switched off the engine. 'I've reserved a table, but we can go somewhere else if you'd rather.'

'I thought you had to book about three years in advance to get in here?' said Jane accusingly, and he grinned suddenly.

'That, Jane, depends who you are!'

When he smiled like that, the years dissolved, and he looked twenty-five again, young, reckless, arrogantly confident about the future. Jane's heart turned over. It was that confidence that had attracted her more than anything else. He had always been so positive, so sure of himself, so different from everyone else in Penbury who liked to be cautious and careful. Lyall wasn't like that. He had dazzled her with his willingness to take risks, carried her along with his certainty that the world outside Penbury offered excitement and success if only she was prepared to grasp them. Only in the end she had stayed, and he had gone, and if he could get a table at a restaurant like this he had obviously found what he was looking for.

The restaurant director himself greeted Lyall with respectful familiarity and led them to a secluded table with a beautiful view out on to the river.

'You should have told me that we were coming here,' Jane whispered to Lyall as they sat down. She was very conscious of the other women in the restaurant, all of whom were immaculately dressed and all of whom seemed to be covertly eyeing Lyall. 'I'm underdressed.'

Lyall opened his menu and considered Jane over the top of it. Ruffled by memories and by finding herself in an unexpected situation, she was looking pink and cross, but her eyes were very bright. The smooth, silky brown hair framed the pure lines of her face and gleamed golden in the light through the window.

'The interesting thing about you, Jane, is that without making any effort at all you manage to make every other woman look *overdressed*,' he said thoughtfully.

Jane stared at him in astonishment, but he had gone back to the menu. Unaccountably flustered, she opened her own, but the words danced in front of her eyes and she had to frown to steady them. The next moment, a waiter was placing a chilled glass of champagne in front of her.

'I thought the occasion called for some celebration,' Lyall explained at her look of mingled suspicion and surprise, and Jane forced herself to sound cool.

'Oh? What exactly are we celebrating?'

'Our reunion?' he suggested.

'This isn't a reunion,' she reminded him crisply. 'This is a business dinner.'

'Is that why you're being so polite?' he asked, amused.

Jane gave him a frosty look. 'I thought that was what you wanted?'

'All I said was that I wanted you to be nice,' said Lyall mildly, and she ruffled up instantly.

'I am being nice!'

'No, you're not. You've been carrying on as if you were at a rather tedious cocktail party and couldn't wait to leave—and believe me, I've been to enough tedious cocktail parties to recognise that kind of trite, meaningless chatter when I hear it!'

Affronted, Jane glared across the table at him. 'Thanks very much! You were the one who said this was going to be a business dinner, if you remember. I'm just treating you as I would any other business acquaintance, which is more than I can say for you—unless you invite all your business contacts out to dinner and then accuse them of being trite when all they're doing is making an effort to do what *you* want because they know that if they don't their livelihood could be at stake!' Grey eyes silver with indignation, she took a defiant gulp of champagne and set the glass back down on the cloth with a sharp click, but to her fury Lyall didn't look in the slightest bit abashed. Instead the blue eyes were regarding her with amused appreciation.

'That's much better, Jane!' he approved. 'At least I can recognise the Jane I once knew now.'

'You're not supposed to be recognising me,' Jane pointed out in frustration, furious with herself for letting him provoke her so easily. 'We agreed last night that we would treat each other as strangers, if you remember.'

'I didn't mean literally. I meant that we should start afresh and try not to let the fact that we had been lovers affect us now.'

'Oh, I *see*,' she said sarcastically. 'So kissing me was just a way of putting the past behind us, was it?'

Lyall's mouth quivered. 'No, I'm afraid it was irresistible,' he said. 'You insisted on paying me and I accepted, that's all. It wasn't so bad, was it?'

Faint colour tinged Jane's cheeks, and she opened her menu with studied casualness. 'I'd rather it didn't happen again.'

'Most people would have been glad to have had their boiler fixed that cheaply,' said Lyall with what Jane suspected was deliberate provocation.

'If I'd known that it was going to cost me a kiss, I'd rather have stuck with a cold bath!'

'Now, now, Jane!' he reproved her, infuriatingly unperturbed. 'You always used to be honest. Can you look me in the eyes, put your hand on your heart and tell me that you didn't enjoy it?'

Jane would have sold her soul to be able to do just that, but Lyall had always had an uncanny ability to read what he had called her 'disastrously honest' eyes. So she kept them fixed firmly on her menu instead. 'You took unfair advantage of the fact that I didn't know who you were, and you know it.'

'Does that mean that you *would* have enjoyed the kiss if you'd known I was chairman of Multiplex?'

'No, it doesn't!' she said with a hostile look. 'It means that I wouldn't have let myself get into that... situation... in the first place.'

'You wouldn't have let me fix your boiler?'

'Of course not!' Jane lowered the menu and looked across at Lyall who was calmly perusing his own as if they were exchanging commonplaces about the weather. 'Why *did* you?'

'Why did I what?'

Her lips tightened. 'Why did you turn up and fix it yourself? You could have bought up a hundred plumbing

firms to send round without even blinking! There was
no need for us to go through that...that *charade*—or
did you deliberately plan to make me look a fool?'

'Don't be melodramatic, Jane,' said Lyall. 'It doesn't
suit you. I didn't *plan* anything. I rang you yesterday
morning because we'd obviously started off on the wrong
foot meeting at Penbury Manor like that. If you remember, you weren't exactly welcoming, and I didn't
think you'd believe me even if I did tell you who I was,
but I'd already made a decision about the contracts and
I thought the next morning that perhaps I ought to warn
you. As it turned out, I didn't get the chance. All I got
was a mouthful of abuse intended for the unfortunate
George Smiles. I decided it would only make matters
worse if I rang back and told you what you'd done, and
anyway, I thought it might be easier to explain face to
face.'

'I didn't notice you doing any explaining when you
got there!' said Jane tartly.

'No, well...you were so damned prickly it was impossible to tell you anything,' he retorted. 'I was working
up to tell you later, when I suggested that we put the
past behind us, but then you insisted on paying me for
fixing the boiler and I got...distracted.'

Distracted! That devastating kiss had turned her whole
world upside-down and he had been *distracted*! Jane
stared fixedly down at the list of dishes without seeing
any of them. All she could see were Lyall's hands holding
his menu, the same hands that had unbuttoned her blouse
last night, the hands that had slid insistently over her
skin, cupping and curving until she had arched towards
him...

She swallowed and forced herself to concentrate on
the menu. She was never going to get through this meal
if she allowed herself to think about that kiss. Fortu-
nately, the head waiter materialised by their table just

then, and by the time they had ordered and the wine list had been discussed she had herself under control again.

'Is there anything else I should know about you that you've been too "distracted" to tell me?' she asked when the waiter had bowed himself off.

'Is there anything else you want to know?' Lyall countered, offering her the plate of exquisite canapés that had been left on the table.

She took one, carefully composed. 'The only thing I want to know is why you've come back to Penbury,' she said.

'You know why,' he shrugged. 'Multiplex has its headquarters in the City, but we've been looking for somewhere out of London as a training and research base. I want a place where scientists and researchers can meet and exchange ideas, where we can run conferences, entertain clients or simply encourage my staff by getting them together with their colleagues from around the world. Just because they all deal with electronics in some way or another, it doesn't mean they won't appreciate the charm and character of a place like Penbury Manor as much as anyone else.'

'That doesn't explain why *you're* here,' said Jane. 'A man in your position doesn't have to go anywhere he doesn't want to, and when you left here ten years ago you said you were never coming back. I just wondered what made you change your mind.'

'It wasn't the need to rediscover my roots, if that's what you're thinking,' said Lyall, and the blue eyes suddenly held a trace of bitterness. 'I cut myself off from them a long time ago. I'm interested in the future, not the past.'

His voice was flat, final, and Jane glanced at him curiously. It occurred to her for the first time how little she knew of Lyall before she had met him. She knew that his mother was dead—it had been one of the few

things they had in common—but she had never been
invited to meet his father. Joe Harding was reputedly a
morose, reclusive man, but Lyall had never talked about
him, and Jane had been too wrapped up in her feelings
for Lyall to ask. Now she wished that she had, but there
was a withdrawn look to Lyall's expression that deterred
further questions. Jane had the distinct impression that
she had trespassed on forbidden territory, and prudently
retreated.

'So...why Penbury now?' she asked, keeping her voice
as light as she could.

Lyall had picked up a fork and was turning it absently
between his fingers, as if he too was thinking reluctantly
about the past, but at her question he seemed to rec-
ollect himself. 'It was a purely business decision,' he said,
replacing the fork. 'Once I'd given the project the go-
ahead, I handed the details over to Dennis. He came up
with a number of possible properties, and Penbury
Manor just happened to be the most suitable.' Picking
up the bottle of wine, he topped up Jane's glass. 'I hadn't
thought about Penbury. As far as I was concerned, I'd
put the place behind me, and it was odd to come across
it in quite a different context. I could have insisted that
Dennis find somewhere else, but I've always kept my
personal feelings quite separate from business, and
coming to Penbury was the right decision from a business
point of view.'

'You didn't need to come yourself,' Jane pointed out.
'You could have let Dennis deal with the renovations.'

'I could have, yes, but, as I said in the meeting this
afternoon, I like to be involved in every aspect of the
firm's activities. There's no point in sitting in some
boardroom making decisions when you don't know
exactly what's going on, and that goes for the development of a base like Penbury Manor will be as much
as for attempting to break into a new market or the start

of a major research project. Any contractor working for me—and that includes you, Jane—needs to realise that this is a priority project and that I won't be satisfied with anything less than the best.'

'Is that why you came down? To make sure we all knew exactly what we were dealing with?'

'Partly. And I was curious too, I must admit. I went to London after I left Penbury, and then to the States. That's where I first got into electronics, and for the next few years I was too committed to building up the company to waste any time thinking about the past. I never thought I'd have any more to do with Penbury, and I was taken aback when I saw the name on Dennis's first report about suitable properties.' He swirled the wine around his glass, frowning down into it as he remembered. 'If anyone had asked me before then, I'd have said that I'd put Penbury behind me, but I began to remember things I thought I'd forgotten. I found myself thinking about fishing in the Pen, or winter mornings with the sheep up on the hills, or the woods behind the manor.' Lifting his eyes from his wine, he looked across the table at Jane sitting slim and straight, her grey eyes guarded. 'And I remembered you,' he added softly. 'I remembered odd things about you, like how you used to turn your head and how the sunlight used to fall through the leaves across your skin.'

Memory prickled over Jane's skin. She could almost feel the warmth of the light, almost smell the dried leaves beneath her feet as she waited in the woods, and her heart began to thud and boom just as it had used to do whenever she had turned to see Lyall coming towards her.

'Did you remember how you broke my heart?' she asked unsteadily, but Lyall only shook his head.

'You broke that yourself. It was nothing to do with me.'

'No, it was nothing to do with you,' said Jane bitterly. 'You just left, and you never came back.'

Lyall put his glass down. 'I did come back,' he said.

She stared at him. 'You came back? When?'

'A few months later. My father died unexpectedly and I came back to sort things out and sell the farm. I'd had time to think things through by then, and I thought you might have done too, so I went over to Penbury to see you and try to explain, but your father told me that you'd gone off to horticultural college and that you never wanted to see me again.' He shrugged. 'I suppose I could have pursued you further, but you'd told me much the same thing, after all. I decided we were better off without each other.'

'He didn't tell me,' said Jane, looking down at her hands and thinking of all the years she had thought that Lyall had never made any effort to contact her again. When she glanced up at him again, her eyes were very dark. 'He should have told me.'

Lost opportunities reverberated in the air between them as they looked at each other, the tension broken only by the arrival of the waiter, who placed the plates reverently in front of them. Jane wasn't hungry, but she was so relieved at the interruption that she picked up her knife and fork with alacrity, pretending an enthusiasm for the beautifully presented dish that she didn't feel. She was still having trouble coming to terms with the fact that her father hadn't told her the one thing he must have known she most wanted to hear.

'Your father probably meant it for the best,' said Lyall, reading her thoughts with uncanny accuracy. 'I didn't like him any more than he liked me, but I suppose he was just trying to protect you, and who are we to say that it *wasn't* for the best?'

'I'm not saying that,' said Jane, lifting her chin. The last thing she wanted was for Lyall to think that she had any regrets! 'I think we both know that it *was* all for the best.'

The blue eyes regarding her held more than a hint of irony. 'Do we?'

'Of course,' she said, pleased with how cool and composed she sounded at last. 'It would have been a terrible mistake if I'd gone away with you. You might never have gone to the States and made a success of Multiplex, and I wouldn't have been doing what *I* want to do.'

'You're not doing what you want to do,' Lyall pointed out unfairly. 'You wanted to be a horticulturist. Instead you're running a building firm.'

'I'm living the way I want to,' said Jane with a cold look.

'Are you? Or are you living the way your father wanted you to? He was the one who wanted you to stay in Penbury and struggle on with the firm.'

'Strange as it may seem to you, I *like* living in Penbury,' she said. 'I like having roots. I like having a garden. I like having friends near by. I wouldn't have had any of those things if I'd gone with you. You would have always wanted to move on, go somewhere different, try something new, and after a while you'd have wanted a new girl too. Commitment never was your thing, was it?'

'I've committed myself to Multiplex,' said Lyall evenly. 'You can't ask for more commitment than that.'

'I was talking personally,' said Jane, toying with a piece of smoked salmon.

'I haven't noticed you being particularly good at personal commitment either,' he said in a cool voice. 'If you feel so strongly about it, why don't you marry your tame solicitor? Judging by the way he was looking at you in the pub the other night, he'd have you like a shot.'

Jane gave up on the salmon and put down her knife and fork. 'Maybe I will,' she said defiantly.

'And maybe you won't. And in the meantime he has to hang on and on until you feel like making up your mind?'

'Marriage is a big step,' she said, on the defensive. 'It's only sensible to wait until you're sure.'

'You call it sensible,' said Lyall. 'I call it cowardly. Either you love him or you don't, and if you do you should take the plunge and get married instead of dithering around and waiting until you're sure someone better isn't going to come along.'

'Why are you so keen on marriage all of a sudden?' demanded Jane suspiciously. 'I didn't think you believed in it?'

'I'm not the one banging on about commitment,' he retorted. 'I'm just suggesting that you practise what you preach, but you'll never do that, will you? You talk a lot about being sensible, but that's just an excuse for never committing yourself to anything. You're in no position to lecture me about commitment, Jane—at least I'm honest about what I want, which is more than can be said for you!'

'Being honest about what you want is just another way of admitting that you're selfish!'

'Perhaps,' he admitted unexpectedly. 'The success of Multiplex has meant that I can go where I want, when I want, and I'm not prepared to give up that freedom. Any woman I get involved with has to accept that. I don't offer marriage. I offer her a wonderful time for as long as we enjoy being together, and if that's not enough that's too bad. I think that's more honest than being sensible, and it's certainly a lot more fun! How much fun do you have with your solicitor?'

Not much. Alan was a good man, a kind man, but he wasn't fun. He didn't make her laugh the way Lyall used to. He didn't make her heart beat faster just by walking into a room, he didn't alarm her or infuriate her and the world didn't seem so bright or so full of possibilities when he was around. But he was safe, Jane reminded herself desperately. He was reliable. He would never break her heart as Lyall had done.

And she would never love him the way she had loved Lyall.

'Sometimes having fun isn't enough,' she said.

CHAPTER FIVE

'IT WAS once, wasn't it, Jane?' Across the table, Lyall's eyes were very blue, and Jane had to steel herself against the recollection of times when love and laughter and the feel of his hand around hers had been all that mattered. It was easy to remember those times and forget that in the end all the happiness had proved illusory.

Her eyes slid away from his and she picked up her glass with a hand that wasn't quite steady. 'I thought we were going to try and put the past behind us?' she said with an edge of desperation.

'It's not that easy, though, is it, Jane?'

No, it wasn't easy. It wasn't easy at all.

'I think we should try, anyway,' she said. 'There's no point in talking about the past.'

Lyall leant back in his chair and regarded her steadily. 'All right, what *shall* we talk about?'

Jane's mind went predictably blank. What *could* they talk about that wouldn't lead straight back to the summer they had shared? 'Tell me how you got started in electronics,' she said after a feverish search had failed to come up with anything better.

Her attempt to sound like the perfect business guest brought an ironic smile to Lyall's eyes, but to her relief he seemed happy to follow her lead and tell her how in ten short years he had transformed a small, struggling electronics factory into a multinational company which produced everything from satellite equipment to the latest in medical technology, to the humbler household tools that made life simpler and easier for the housewife. 'Our main interests are in America and Europe,' he finished, 'but we've got subsidiaries all round the world now, and I'm in the middle of trying to set up a deal with the Japanese that should consolidate our position in the Far East.'

It was an impressive story, but Jane was determined not to let him know that she thought so. Lyall had gone a long way since he left Penbury. 'It sounds as if you spend your whole time travelling,' she commented in a neutral voice. 'Don't you have a home?'

'I've got several,' he said ironically. 'I don't particularly like hotels, so Multiplex owns a number of apartments around the world which I use when I'm travelling.'

'Owning an apartment isn't the same as having a home, is it?' said Jane.

Lyall hunched a shoulder. 'The idea of home is overrated as far as I'm concerned,' he said flatly. 'I had a home for the first seventeen years of my life and I didn't think much of it. I suppose I spend most time at my flat in London, but it's really just somewhere to sleep. I don't want to be tied to any one place any more than I do to any one person.'

'In that case, I'm surprised you're so keen to have your own apartments in Penbury Manor,' she said, wondering at his bitter reference to the farm where he had grown up. She wished she had known more about his family life. She wished she had asked.

'I'll have to stay somewhere when I come down,' he pointed out. 'There doesn't seem to be any point in buying another property which I'll only use when I'm visiting the manor.'

'I suppose not.' Jane ran her finger around the rim of her glass.

'You're looking a little wistful, Jane,' said Lyall, and she sighed.

'Oh...I was just thinking about Penbury Manor and how it's going to change. If I owned it, I certainly wouldn't turn it into a conference centre and convert a few rooms just so that I didn't have to stay in the pub whenever I came down!'

'I suppose you'd keep everybody out and spend all day in the garden?' he said caustically, and Jane gave a wry smile.

'I suppose it would be just as much of a waste,' she acknowledged, with another little sigh. 'What that house really needs is a family to live in it and love it.' She had spoken without really thinking, but when she glanced up from her glass she found Lyall watching her with a curiously intent expression, and for some unaccountable reason she blushed.

'I can't provide a family,' he said drily. 'But you'll be pleased to know that I *have* done something about the rose garden.'

Jane, still fighting the blush, looked at him blankly. 'The rose garden?'

'The rose garden you were so concerned about that day we met at the manor,' he explained with humiliating patience. 'You were furious at the idea of building a research lab on top of it, remember?'

Trust him to remind her of that! 'What about it?' she asked suspiciously.

'If you hadn't walked out of the meeting this afternoon, you'd have heard that I've arranged for the lab to be built somewhere else, so the most your precious roses will have to face is a severe prune, which, judging by the state they're in, shouldn't do them any harm!'

'You're going to keep the rose garden after all?' Jane could hardly believe what she was hearing.

'You don't sound very pleased,' Lyall complained. 'I thought you'd be delighted.'

'I am . . . I'm just surprised, that's all. What made you change your mind?'

'It wasn't the right place for the lab anyway,' he said gruffly, but when his eyes met hers they held a smile and Jane found herself smiling back at him as if he'd changed his mind because he knew that it would please her.

'Thank you,' she said.

There was a moment of utter stillness as they looked at each other, smiles slowly fading. Jane felt as if she and Lyall were marooned in a circle of silence, isolated from the chink and chatter of the restaurant by a steadily tightening band of awareness. She wanted to look away, but she couldn't. She couldn't move, couldn't speak, couldn't remember how much he had hurt her. All she could do was look into his dark blue eyes and remember how it had felt when he'd kissed her.

Once she had allowed herself to remember, it was impossible to forget. Somehow Jane got through the rest of the meal, but afterwards she had no recollection of what they had talked about. She was too aware of Lyall sitting opposite her, of his fingers curled around his glass, of his mouth, of the way her heart jarred and the polite, constrained conversation faltered whenever their eyes met.

Roses meant nothing to Lyall. How many times had he accused her of caring more for plants than for people? 'You only like plants because you know where you are with them,' he used to say. 'They can't get up and walk away because they're stuck in the ground, just as you'd like to be.' Had he given the rose garden a reprieve because of her, or had it really just been because it was the wrong site for the laboratory? Jane felt confused, uncertain. She wanted to convince herself that it didn't matter either way, but whenever she thought she had she would catch a glimpse of Lyall's mouth and her heart would turn over.

The meal seemed to last forever but at last it was over and they were walking back to the car. It was a soft summer night, and the sky was a deep, dusky blue, still not quite dark. The lights from the restaurant glimmered on the still river and the murmur of voices, interspersed with laughter, drifted out through the open windows. Jane was agonisingly conscious of Lyall walking easily beside her. His white shirt gleamed in contrast to his dark jacket and in the shadowy light there was something overwhelmingly solid about him. Glancing sideways at him, she was engulfed by a sudden, terrifying urge to touch him, to feel the strength of his muscles beneath his jacket, beneath the sleek skin she remembered so well.

Appalled at the force of her desire, Jane wrapped her arms around herself, as if afraid that her hands might stray of their own accord, but it didn't do any good. She couldn't stop thinking about the last time he had made love to her in the woods. His body had been strong and supple and searingly warm. She had wrapped herself around him, loving the feel of him, the taste of him, while he had explored her with a tantalising lack of haste, his hands slow and sure on her skin.

The memory shuddered down to the base of her spine where it clenched so savagely that Jane almost gasped. Lyall saw her shiver and frowned.

'Are you cold?'

She swallowed. 'A little.' It was a good enough excuse although the night was warm and inside she was on fire.

They drove back to Penbury in virtual silence. Jane gripped her hands together in her lap and sought frantically for something to say, but her mind refused to function as instructed, and kept veering back to Lyall's mouth, to the warmth of his kisses and the hardness of his body and the intoxicating excitement of his touch. It was impossible to tell what Lyall was thinking. In the

reflected glow of the dashboard, his face was preoccupied, apparently intent on the road ahead, but every
now and then he would glance across at her, inevitably
at the very moment when she had decided to risk a look
at him, and their eyes would meet jarringly before flickering quickly away while the atmosphere tightened
another screw.

Never had Jane been so relieved to see the sign pointing
down the narrow lane to Penbury. Lyall had barely
stopped the car outside the house before she had leapt
out and fled to the safety of her gate, turning to face
him only when she had shut it firmly between them.

'Thank you for a delicious meal,' she said, horribly
conscious that her voice sounded two octaves higher than
usual.

'I'm glad you enjoyed it,' said Lyall with equal for-
mality. It was hard to read his expression in the darkness,
even though he was standing very close and there was
only the gate between them, but Jane was humiliatingly
certain that she could hear that dangerous smile back in
his voice.

She clutched the wooden bar as if to reassure herself
that it was still there. 'Well...goodnight,' she managed,
and took a step back, only to find herself brought up
short by Lyall's hand closing unhurriedly around her
wrist. Curving his other hand against her face, he pulled
her slowly, inexorably back towards him until she was
pressed against the gate and he was smoothing the hair
away from her face.

'Goodnight, Jane,' he said softly, and bent his head
to capture her lips with his own.

She just had time to brace herself against the electrifying touch of his mouth, but it didn't make much dif-
ference. His kiss was so warm, so tantalisingly persuasive
that her resistance dissolved in a wash of sheer pleasure,
and she melted against him for one betraying moment

before her mind shrieked at her belatedly to push him away and she dragged herself reluctantly up out of the rush of sensation.

Lifting her hands to his chest, she felt her fingers curl treacherously around the lapels of his jacket and it took a huge effort of will to spread them and pull back, her eyes wide and dark and torn with shameful longing.

Lyall let her go easily. Jane's hands shook as she scrabbled in her bag for her keys. Take it lightly. Don't let him know that you've been thinking about that all the way home. Don't let him know how much you want him to pull you back into his arms.

'Are you planning to kiss all your contractors after you've taken them out to dinner?' she asked as steadily as she could.

Lyall's smile gleamed suddenly through the darkness. 'Not unless they've got skin like silk and the clearest grey eyes I've ever seen,' he said, and turned calmly back to his car. 'Goodnight, Jane,' he said again over the roof. 'I'll see you around.'

Dear Jane,
    Wonderful news! Carmelita and I got married last week. I know you'll be happy for me. Everything is perfect here, but could you send me some more money? Married life is proving expensive! Love, Kit.

Jane read the card for the fifth time before dropping it on to the hall table with a tiny sigh. Her little brother, married! She had been eleven when their mother died, Kit six years younger, and she had stepped naturally in to a mother's role, making his bed, cooking his breakfast, making sure he had clean clothes. Later it had been Jane to whom Kit had turned when he was short of money or wanted a lift late at night. Effortlessly charming, always restlessly searching for new excitements, he had at times reminded Jane painfully of Lyall, and she had been more than usually understanding of the distraught girls who used to turn up on the doorstep wanting to know why Kit had disappeared without a word.

Now it seemed that Kit had settled down at last, just as their father had always wanted. Kit had mentioned Carmelita a couple of times in his erratic postcards, but there had been no indication that she was any more serious than all the others. And now they were married.

Jane couldn't help feeling hurt as she drove up to Penbury Manor to check on the progress of the renovations. It was typical of Kit that he couldn't even be bothered to write her a letter to tell her about his marriage, and that the casual news had been coupled with a request for money. He treated Makepeace and Son like his own personal bank, and never gave a thought to where the money was coming from. Jane had tried to explain about budgets and overdrafts and cash-flow problems when he'd come back for their father's funeral, but it had gone in one ear and out the other. Kit knew perfectly well that he could rely on his elder sister. She had never let him down before.

She would have to find some money from somewhere, Jane thought, blind for once to the tranquil beauty of the countryside. Her father would certainly have given Kit something when he married. Perhaps she could get a loan now that they had the Penbury Manor contract. They had only been working there for three weeks and there was still a long way to go before they would be paid.

Still pondering the problem, she swung the van into the drive, but all thoughts of Kit were driven from her head as soon as she saw Lyall's car parked on the gravel forecourt, Dimity Price's smart little hatchback tucked cosily beside it.

So he was back.

Jane's heart began cartwheeling crazily and she had to take a deep, steadying breath before she got out of the van. She hadn't seen Lyall since he had driven off and left her clutching her keys behind the gate that night. She should have been glad, of course, but it had annoyed her to find herself looking round corners, never knowing when he was suddenly going to reappear. It had left her feeling unaccountably grumpy and on edge. It wasn't that she wanted to see Lyall—it was definitely not *that*!—but it would have been less unsettling if only she knew when to expect him. Of course it was typical of Lyall to kiss her and then disappear, leaving her to wonder whether it had indeed just been a business dinner as far as he was concerned. It was equally typical of him to reappear just when she had decided that since he obviously wasn't coming back she could relax.

Jane clamped ruthlessly down on her treacherously gyrating heart as she walked over the gravel. At least his car had given her some warning of his reappearance. This would be her chance to show him how totally unmoved she had been by that last goodnight kiss. If he thought she had spent the last three weeks waiting for him to contact her again, she would be more than happy to disabuse him!

She saw Lyall and Dimity as soon as she let herself into the hall. They were standing close together by the window-seat in the library. The door was open, and they were looking through books of sample fabrics, so absorbed in what they were doing that they were unaware of Jane's unwilling gaze. Dimity kept running her hand through her flowing curls and trilling with laughter, and as Jane watched Lyall turned his head and smiled down at her.

Something cold closed around Jane's heart. Turning on her heel, she marched up the stairs to find Ray, who was acting as foreman at the manor. So what if Lyall smiled at other girls just the way he smiled at her? *She* didn't care. No doubt it had amused him to take her out and stir her up just the way he used to, but he was clearly lining Dimity up to entertain him during this visit.

Well, good. That would keep him out of *her* hair.

Jane found Ray in the bathroom that Lyall wanted fixed up temporarily so that he could use it while the rest of the house was being restored. For a time they discussed whether it was worth patching up the rusty, leaking pipes that festooned the room, or whether it would be better simply to rip them all out and start again.

'I suppose I'd better ask Mr Harding,' sighed Jane at last, chewing her thumb as she frowned up at the pipes. She had been hoping to leave without talking to Lyall at all.

'Ask me what?'

Jane and Ray swung round to see Lyall lounging in the doorway. He was dressed with easy style in a pale linen jacket and his hands were thrust into the pockets of his comfortable trousers. Jane was grateful for the earlier glimpse of him that enabled her to school her features to what she hoped was bored indifference now.

'We were just wondering what you want to do about the plumbing in here,' she said, pleased at how cool and collected she sounded.

'What's the problem?' he asked, and listened carefully as Ray explained the choice. 'You're the expert,' he said to Ray when he had finished. 'What would you recommend?'

'I'd have it all out,' said Ray without hesitation, and Lyall spread his hands as he turned back to Jane.

'There you are. Decision made. You didn't need to ask me at all.'

'You've changed your tune, haven't you?' said Jane with a sour look. 'I thought you wanted to be involved in every stage of the restoration?'

'That doesn't mean you have to check every detail with me,' said Lyall. 'I just like to know what's happening in general.' He caught up with Jane, who had told Ray that she would see him later and had set off down the long corridor, her footsteps echoing on the bare floorboards. 'What about some lunch?'

'I'm busy,' she said curtly without stopping.

Lyall sighed, but there was an undercurrent of reluctant amusement in his voice. 'Haven't you ever heard of public relations, Jane? I thought we'd agreed that as I'm your most important client you were going to make an effort to be nice to me?'

'I've *been* nice to you,' Jane objected. 'I even went out to dinner with you.'

'That was ages ago.'

'So what? There was nothing in the contract about providing a continuous free escort service!'

'No, but I hoped you'd grasped the principle of not alienating your client if you could help it,' said Lyall smoothly.

Jane stopped abruptly, grey eyes bright with defiance. 'Is that another way of saying that renewing the contract depends on whether I'm prepared to put myself at your beck and call?'

'No, Jane. It's a way of suggesting that we discuss the progress of the work over lunch like two civilised people.'

'Another of your *business* meals?' said Jane acidly.

'Why not?'

'You promised that dinner three weeks ago would be purely business, and look what happened!'

The dark blue eyes were gleaming. 'We had a meal and then I took you home. Would you have preferred a taxi?'

'I would have *preferred* not to be kissed,' said Jane with a frosty look.

'Well, if I promise not to kiss you again, will you come and have some lunch?' said Lyall, evidently more amused than perturbed by Jane's hostility. He smiled down at her, that same smile he had always used to get his own way. There had been a time when Jane's sternest resistance to his more outrageous ideas had crumbled before that smile, but today Lyall's easy charm and certainty that everyone would fall over themselves to do what he wanted grated on her nerves. It reminded her too much of Kit, whose casual announcement of his marriage had left her more hurt than she cared to admit. She was fed up with being taken for granted by men who thought that all they had to do was smile and she would fall at their feet.

'I've got too much to do,' she said tightly, and turned for the stairs leading up to the attics. 'If you want to know how things are going, I suggest you read the weekly progress reports I send to your office. It wouldn't take a whole lunch to tell you that everything's going to plan.'

She had hoped to sound crushing, but Lyall didn't even have the grace to look disappointed at her refusal. 'Well, it was just a thought,' he said casually. 'But if you're so determined to busy, you can come and give me some professional advice.'

Jane stopped with her foot on the first step. 'What about?' she asked suspiciously.

'Dimity's keen to give me her initial ideas for decorating the bedrooms. I thought it would be helpful if you came around at the same time so that we don't get involved in any impractical ideas at the start.'

'That's the architect's job,' said Jane, determinedly unhelpful.

'I know, but I've just had a message saying that Michael White won't be able to make it. It was too late to stop Dimity coming, so rather than waste the opportunity Michael suggested that you would have just as good an idea of what was practical and what wasn't. That's why I was looking for you in the first place.'

'Oh,' she said. So he hadn't just wanted to ask her out to lunch. Why hadn't he said that in the first place? She was tempted to refuse—Lyall was more than capable of spotting impractical ideas, after all!—but, having taken her stand over lunch, she thought it wise not to push him any further. 'Oh, very well,' she said grudgingly. 'Just let me see whether the men on the roof need anything and then I'll come down.'

'Don't be long,' said Lyall, an unmistakable note of warning beneath the lazy humour. It was nearly enough to make Jane linger with the men in the attics deliberately, but she didn't need Lyall to remind her that she couldn't afford to risk losing the contract again, and she made her way reluctantly downstairs.

She found Lyall and Dimity at last in the old picture gallery. Dimity was looking extravagantly pretty in a sweeping, flowered skirt and a lacy top that would have looked ridiculous on anyone else. Next to her daintiness, Jane felt clumsy and dull in her neat striped trousers and the sensible dark blue sweatshirt she wore when visiting sites.

Dimity didn't look over-pleased to hear that Jane was to accompany them on their tour of the bedrooms, but she brightened when Lyall explained why. 'It must be marvellous to be so *practical*,' she said, with a tinkling little laugh. 'I'm afraid I'm hopeless at that kind of thing. Once I've got a vision of how things should be, I get carried away and I simply *can't* be distracted by boring things like pipes or electricity points.'

Having effectively reduced Jane to the same boringly practical category as plumbing, Dimity smiled sweetly and bore Lyall off to the west wing. Jane was left to trail along behind as Dimity wafted around the house, going into paroxysms of delight as they inspected the damp, dilapidated rooms.

'Can't you just *feel* the ghosts?' she cried to Lyall. 'I'm so excited about bringing this wonderful old place back to life.' She glanced under her impossibly long lashes at Jane, who was wistfully remembering how quiet and peaceful the manor had been when Miss Partridge lived there. 'Jane's amazing, isn't she, Lyall?' she said insincerely. 'I wish I could be that cool about it all.'

Lyall had been watching Jane's unconsciously wistful face too. His expression was inscrutable. 'Amazing,' he agreed.

Certain that they were both patronising her, Jane stuck her hands fiercely into her pockets and lifted her chin. They obviously thought that she was just a clod-hopping philistine, not creative enough to appreciate beauty or history or romance. Well, if that was how they saw her, that was how she would be!

'I see this as a symphony of blue and green,' Dimity was saying breathily, throwing open a door into what had once been known as the Red Room from its wall-paper, now tattered and fading.

'What do you see, Jane?' The odd note had disappeared from Lyall's voice and it held only lazy amusement as he enjoyed the contrast between the two girls.

'Damp patches, a dripping radiator and rotten floor-boards,' said Jane briefly. She wasn't about to start competing with Dimity in the femininity stakes. 'We'll need to sort all those out before we can start on the symphony.'

Dimity looked smug, delighted that Jane was merely confirming how prosaically unromantic she was, and floated off, but Lyall lingered, studying Jane with blue, speculative eyes. 'I thought you knew more about gardening than about building?'

'I do, but it doesn't take a genius to see what needs to be done. It's so obvious that I'd have thought it might even occur to Dimity to bother her pretty little head about it.' She knew she sounded catty, but she didn't care. She didn't see why she should have to provide free entertainment for them both.

Dimity, glancing over her shoulder, was put out to discover that Lyall had stayed to talk to Jane instead of following her, and the breathy, little-girl voice sounded positively firm as she called his attention back.

'I thought we could have an *en-suite* bathroom over here,' she said, tossing back her curls. 'Also in blue and green, of course... a sort of marine theme.'

'Hmm.' Lyall didn't sound entirely convinced. He cocked an eyebrow at Jane. 'What do you think?'

Jane was delighted to tell him. 'It's a ridiculous idea,' she said acidly. 'One, that's a supporting wall, so you can't play around with it. Two, even if it weren't, it would mean putting in another window, which would be totally out of keeping. And three, we're nowhere near the sea, which makes the whole idea of a nautical theme affected and silly.'

Dimity's sweet expression froze at this unexpected counter-attack, but she recovered swiftly. 'Oh, Jane, you *meanie*,' she pouted. 'Must you be quite so down-to-earth? Honestly, you should have been a man! Now you've quite ruined all my plans!'

'I thought that was what I was here for,' said Jane coolly, and turned to confront Lyall. 'Isn't it?'

'One of the reasons,' he agreed blandly, but his eyes glinted with laughter and Jane scowled. What was so funny?

'Shall we get on with it, then?' she snapped, heading for the door. 'I haven't got all day to hang around up here.'

The last room they looked at had been labelled for Lyall's personal use on the plan. Jane stalked over to the window and folded her arms impatiently while Dimity twirled around, effusively pointing out different features that Lyall could presumably see perfectly well for himself.

'Now, *this* I see as a very masculine room, to suit your personality,' she gushed, with a coy look at Lyall beneath her lashes. 'I thought it should be dark and dramatic. The terracotta-reds can look marvellous...in fact, I can show you exactly the colours I have in mind.' She tripped off to fetch one of the sample books she had left in the library, and Lyall strolled over to join Jane at the open window.

'Any objections to the dark and dramatic?'

Jane looked down at the once magnificent topiary, now badly in need of clipping, and tried not to notice how close he was. He was leaning forward, resting his hands on the windowsill where they just caught the corner of her vision. She found herself looking at them, as if she had never seen them before, long brown fingers with clean, square-cut nails, and her eyes rested as if fascinated on the grooves across his knuckles and the tendons in the back of his hands before drifting of their own volition up to his face. Laughter-lines were starred around his eyes, their effect offset by the determined set of his jaw and the hint of ruthlessness at his mouth. Jane's own mouth dried just looking at it, and she was caught unprepared when Lyall turned his head and met her clear gaze.

For a long moment they just looked at each other, Jane's expression torn and troubled, his oddly unreadable, before a smile crept back into his eyes. 'Well?' he prompted.

Well? With an effort, Jane recalled his question, and edged away as casually as she could, hoping that Lyall hadn't noticed the blush creeping along her cheeks. 'I've got a feeling this room faces east,' she managed, marvelling at the steadiness in her voice. 'It would be a shame to waste the morning sun by making the room too dark.'

'Good point,' said Lyall. 'It ought to be easy enough to tell what direction it faces. Where's the sun now?' He pushed the window out as far as it would go and before Jane had a chance to protest he had leant right out to squint up at the roof above them.

Without thinking, Jane's hand shot out to grab his jacket. 'Don't *do* that!' she shouted.

Lyall withdrew his head in surprise. 'What's the matter?' His eyes sharpened uncomfortably as his gaze dropped from Jane's face to where her fingers still clutched at his jacket. 'Don't say you were worried about me!' he teased softly.

Jane's cheeks flamed and she whipped her hand away from his jacket as if it had stung her. The feel of his body beneath the linen was burned into her fingers where they had brushed against his side. 'You could have fallen,' she muttered.

'I was only leaning out of the window,' Lyall pointed out. 'Hardly a death-defying stunt!'

'It's just stupid to risk an accident to find out something we could have discovered just as easily by looking at the plans.' Jane was mortified with herself for clutching at him like some frantic lover, and she folded her arms defensively across her chest.

'I'm the impatient type,' he said. 'As you, Jane, know very well. I learnt a long time ago that you don't get anything from this life unless you're prepared to take risks. That was one lesson you never learnt, did you?'

CHAPTER SIX

JANE'S eyes were clear and direct. 'I've never believed in taking risks just for the sake of it,' she agreed evenly. 'Was it so important to find out whether the room faced east or not right now?'

'Why not?' The hard look of memory vanished and Lyall smiled suddenly, unfairly. 'I wasn't in the slightest danger of falling, and I discovered that it does in fact face east, so now you can tell me how you think it should be decorated.'

'It's got nothing to do with me,' grumbled Jane, unsettled by his smile. 'You're supposed to be the tough businessman. You must be used to making your own decisions.'

'I am,' he said. 'But, unlike you, I'm always prepared to listen to good advice.' She had turned her face away, but she could still feel his smile flickering over her skin as if it had a warmth and a light of its own. 'So come on, Jane. You've been giving a very good impression of a practical builder, but I know you're not nearly as practical as you like to pretend. Tell me what you really think.'

Jane sighed and gave in. Turning, she studied the room carefully, admiring its fine proportions. Even dusty and neglected as it was, it was still a light, welcoming room whose quirky fireplace and strange carvings only added to its attractions. It was the sort of room you could never get tired of, she thought a little wistfully, and in the mornings the sunshine would pour in through the two windows.

'I think it will be a lovely room to wake up in,' she said at last, thoroughly unnerved by how clearly she could imagine sleeping in a big bed here, stretching luxuriously in the morning light, opening her eyes to a smiling blue gaze, reaching out for a warm, strong body...

'Ah, but will it be the sort of room you'd like to go to bed in?' Lyall murmured with that uncanny ability he seemed to have to read her thoughts, and Jane stepped back abruptly.

'You should ask Dimity that, not me,' she said shortly, relieved for once to see the other girl come fluttering back into the room with the sample books, full of apologies for taking so long.

'What was it you needed to ask me?' she said at last with an inviting look at Lyall.

The warm blue gaze rested speculatively on Jane for a moment, then he turned to Dimity. 'Why don't I explain over lunch?' he suggested smoothly. 'I know Jane is anxious to get on, but you're free, aren't you, Dimity?'

'Of course,' she gasped, abandoning her sample books. 'I'd simply *adore* to! Let me just go and get my bag from the gallery.'

She tripped excitedly away. Not for the world would Jane have admitted the sense of desolation that swept over her at the realisation that Lyall hadn't particularly cared which girl he took out to lunch. He waited by the door, hands casually in his pockets, looking down the corridor for Dimity's return. As the little footsteps hurried back, he looked across at Jane. 'Don't work too hard,' he said, and went out to meet Dimity, leaving Jane standing alone in the middle of a room which felt cold and empty without him.

The murmur of their voices receded along the corridor, interspersed with Dimity's little trills of laughter. Determined not to follow them, Jane swung on her heel and marched over to the window instead, but it only afforded a perfect view of Lyall solicitously helping Dimity into his car.

She ought to feel glad that he had been so ready to accept her refusal of his invitation to lunch, Jane told herself, watching Dimity's extravagant gestures of gratitude with a jaundiced eye. The trouble was that she didn't feel glad. She felt dreary and disconsolate and inexplicably peeved at having got what she wanted.

And hungry.

In spite of what she had told Lyall, there was nothing to do here. None of the men needed anything and they would be breaking off any minute for their lunch. Jane didn't usually eat anything in the middle of the day, but today it seemed as if everyone was going to be tucking into lunch except her. Lyall had driven off with Dimity, no doubt to some other exclusive restaurant where he would be fawned over by the waiters and they could enjoy a delicious and unjustifiably expensive meal. Jane watched them drive off and then walked dispiritedly down the stairs and out to her old van. She would pick up a sandwich on her way back to the office in Starbridge.

The prospect only made her feel even drearier. On an impulse, she stopped off at Alan's office. He was delighted to see her, but made no effort to hide his surprise when she suggested going out for lunch.

'I didn't think you liked lunch!'

'I don't usually, but...well, I was passing and thought it might be nice for a change.'

It was obvious that Alan took her unexpected appearance as an encouraging sign. Normally he hated spontaneous decisions, but today he closed his files with alacrity and fussed around her. Ignoring Jane's protests that she had only meant a ploughman's lunch in the pub, he insisted on sweeping her across to the Starbridge Hotel.

With its imposing façade and air of traditional grandeur, the Starbridge had long been *the* hotel in the town and was very popular with visitors, who used it as a base for exploring the Cotswolds. Jane had always felt vaguely intimidated by its hushed, expensive atmosphere and was relieved when Alan steered her firmly away from the over-priced dining-room and out to the less formal bistro-style restaurant in the conservatory.

'We must do this more often,' he said to Jane when they were settled. 'Now that I know you can be lured out at lunchtime, I can see you without driving all the way out to Penbury.'

Jane's heart sank. She was fond of Alan, but her heart never missed a beat when she was with him, and it wasn't really fair to encourage him just because she was unsettled by Lyall. 'Today's an exception,' she reminded him firmly.

'Well, in that case I must make the most of your company,' said Alan with the rather old-fashioned, laboured gallantry that was so typical of him. Since his idea of making the most of Jane's company was to launch into a long and boringly detailed account of an obscure legal problem that was currently occupying him, Jane's attention began to wander. Sipping her spritzer, she let her eyes drift around the room while she nodded and smiled and made understanding noises.

There were a surprising number of people sitting among the potted plants. Having lived in the area all her life, Jane recognised several of them, and she was just wondering whether that could really be Billy Tate, the naughtiest boy at primary school, in a respectable suit and tie, when her eyes moved on, only to jar to a sickening halt as they locked with a blazing blue gaze.

What was Lyall doing *here*?

For a long, jangling moment they stared at each other across the room, and then Lyall looked deliberately away. Jane felt as if she had been slapped. She put down her glass so unsteadily that half the wine slipped over the edge and Alan, who hadn't even noticed that he had lost her attention at all, reached across to mop up the spill with his napkin and tried not to look put out at the interruption.

Why couldn't they have gone to the pub as she had wanted? Jane tried to concentrate on what Alan was saying, but she was overwhelmingly conscious of Lyall on the other side of the room. She felt oddly shaken by the fierce look in his eyes, but whenever she slid a covert glance across the room he and Dimity were having an uproarious time together and she decided she must have imagined that blaze of something that could almost have been jealousy.

To prove that she didn't care in the least whether Lyall was jealous or not, Jane smiled brilliantly at Alan and hoped that if Lyall was able to drag his attention away from Dimity for a second he would be able to see just how much she was enjoying herself having lunch with someone else.

Gratified by Jane's sudden intense interest in his career, Alan expanded considerably and it wasn't long before he was dropping heavy hints about putting their relationship on a different footing. 'We've known each other a long time now, haven't we?' he said, taking her hand. 'Don't you think it's time we got married? I know you don't want to rush into anything but we could at least get engaged. You know that it's what I want.'

Jane tugged her hand away. 'I'll have to think about it,' she temporised, burningly aware of Lyall on the other side of the room.

'You will?' Alan's face brightened. It was more than Jane had ever promised before. 'Promise?'

'I'm not promising anything,' said Jane hurriedly. She felt awful. The last thing she had wanted to do was encourage Alan!

'Oh, I know that,' he said eagerly, recapturing her hand. 'But still, you *will* think about it?'

'Hel-*lo*!' Dimity's fluting voice interrupted them and Jane's head jerked up even as her heart sank. Dimity had clearly been delighted to see that Jane had a companion. Jane was convinced that she had dragged Lyall over to make sure that he realised she was out of the running, though why she should have bothered Jane couldn't imagine. She was hardly a rival to Dimity's frilly femininity.

Lyall's expression was sardonic. He looked down at the table where Jane's hand still lay beneath Alan's, then he looked at Alan. He didn't say a word, but to Jane's chagrin Alan immediately withdrew his hand, leaving hers marooned conspicuously in the middle of the table, and her colour rose.

'Hello,' she said coldly.

Dimity was cooing about what an am*a*zing coincidence it was to meet Jane again so soon. 'Hardly amazing,' said Jane in a crisp voice, deciding that of all the things that most irritated her about Dimity her habit of stressing odd syllables had to be the worst. Starbridge isn't a very big place.' She glanced at Lyall. 'I'm surprised to see *you* here, though,' she went on, thinking of the five-star restaurant he had taken her to before. 'The Starbridge Hotel isn't exactly your style. Isn't it a little unpretentious for you?'

His eyes narrowed at her tone. 'The surprise is in seeing *you*, surely? I thought you were busy?'

'I'm never too busy to see Alan,' Jane found herself saying. She directed a dazzling smile across at Alan who managed to look smug and surprised at the same time, and then risked another glance at Lyall, pleased to see his brows snap together.

'Aren't you going to introduce us?' he growled, although he must have known perfectly well who Alan was.

Jane made the introductions grudgingly, and only Dimity appeared to be as pleased as they all said they were. It was obvious that Alan hadn't taken to Lyall, but as ever he was punctiliously polite. 'Jane's told me all about you, of course,' he said as he shook Lyall's hand reluctantly.

'Has she?' Lyall's eyes gleamed as he glanced provocatively at Jane. '*All* about me?'

'Naturally I've told Alan about Multiplex and the work we're doing at the manor,' she said stiffly. She had never told Alan about that long-ago affair with Lyall. She didn't think it was something he would understand. She met Lyall's gaze directly, daring him to tell the truth. He wouldn't do that, though, she was sure. Telling Alan would mean telling Dimity too, and she didn't think he would want that.

'I understand that it's going to be a sort of research centre,' said Alan, clearly suspicious of the almost tangible tension that existed between Jane and Lyall. 'I don't suppose you'll be spending much time down here yourself.'

'Oh, I don't know,' said Lyall surprisingly. 'I'm sure Jane will have told you that I'm setting aside a set of apartments for my own use. I may well end up spending quite a lot of time down here.'

Jane stared at him uneasily. 'But you said you'd only use the apartment occasionally once the work was finished!'

'Did I?' Lyall smiled his enjoyment of her dismay. 'Perhaps I've changed my mind. I'm beginning to wonder whether there's more to keep me in Penbury than

I originally thought.' And, taking Dimity by the arm, he wished them both a steely goodbye and walked out, leaving his words echoing behind him like a threat.

Alan scowled after him. 'I didn't like the way that chap looked at you,' he said sullenly to Jane.

'What do you mean, the way he looked at me?'

'I don't know... as if you belonged to him in some way. I got the distinct impression that he didn't like me holding your hand, anyway!' He chewed his lower lip petulantly. 'There's nothing between you two, is there?'

'Of course not,' said Jane coldly. 'If you must know, I can't stand the man, and even if I could it's pretty obvious that he's only interested in that Dimity Price. Why else do you think he's planning to spend more time down here?'

Alan's brow cleared. 'You think he's involved with her? I suppose she *is* very pretty. Much too sweet to get mixed up with a man like that, anyway.' He seemed to realise that he might have sounded a little too enthusiastic about Dimity and caught Jane's hand once more. 'What does it matter, anyway? As long as he's not interested in *you*! See how jealous I am with you, darling!'

Jane forced a smile and tried to tug her hand free. 'I really must go,' she said, feeling guilty at having encouraged Alan as much as she had. If it hadn't been for Lyall's standing there and having the nerve to look thunderous just because Alan was holding her hand, she would never have said that about never being too busy to spend time with Alan. If it hadn't been for Lyall, she would never have suggested this wretched lunch in the first place, and if Lyall hadn't been distracting her on the other side of the room she wouldn't have told Alan she would even think about getting engaged. It was all Lyall's fault!

'You'll think about what we talked about, though?' Alan insisted, still hanging on to her hand. 'You'll think about how happy we would be if we were married?'

What could she say? She could hardly explain to him now that she had only encouraged him because of Lyall. 'All right, I'll think about it,' she promised with an inward sigh.

Jane always kept her promises. She *did* think about it. Alone in her garden that evening, she sat and imagined what it would be like to be married to Alan. He would mow the lawn and check the oil in the car and make sure that all the bills were paid on time—all things that Jane was more than capable of doing herself. He would be faithful, considerate, utterly reliable. She would never have to wonder where he was or what he was doing. Really, he would be an ideal husband, she tried to tell herself. Only when an ideal husband kissed her she wouldn't close her eyes and see only a pair of glinting blue eyes. She didn't even know what colour Alan's eyes were, Jane realised guiltily. All she knew was that they weren't like Lyall's. His mouth wasn't like Lyall's and his hands weren't like Lyall's and her bones didn't melt whenever he kissed her.

The next time she met Alan, Jane tried to tell him gently that she thought it would be best if they just stayed friends. Unfortunately, he refused to be convinced that she meant what she said. He seemed to think that by promising to think about getting engaged she had accepted the idea in principle, and that all that was left to do was buy a ring. Jane's protestations that he had misunderstood her simply bounced off him. Impervious to every argument, he merely patted her hand and told her she just needed time to get used to the idea. Jane began to feel trapped. She was obviously going to have to be brutally honest with him, but she kept putting it off.

Alan would feel hurt and humiliated and she already felt guilty enough about having encouraged him unfairly.

Jane sighed as she walked through Penbury woods one evening about a week after that wretched lunch. Alan was getting so persistent that she had taken to making excuses about seeing him, or, as now, contriving to be out of the house when he was likely to ring. The woods had always been her refuge. It was here that she had come when Lyall had left, and again when her father had died. Whenever the responsibility of running the firm or worry about Kit got too much, she would come up and be soothed by the gnarled old trees and the soft, dappled light. She wished she could stop feeling guilty about Alan. She had enough to think about trying to find some money to send to Kit. Another postcard had arrived telling her about the wonderful apartment he and Carmelita could move into if only they had the money, and Jane was afraid that the only way she could raise enough cash was to sell the house. It was a prospect that filled her with dread, and she kept putting off the call to the estate agent. She sighed. Perhaps it was better to think about Alan after all.

It hadn't rained for a few days now, but there were still some muddy patches in the deepest shade, and Jane had to pick her way carefully. Wandering slowly along the path, she tried to rehearse a speech that would convince Alan that she couldn't marry him, but her mental excuses kept getting tangled up with thoughts of Lyall: the laughter that lurked in his eyes sometimes as he looked down at her, the way he annoyed her and unsettled her and tied her up in knots, the way her senses spun out of control when he kissed her. Whenever she thought about *that* her stomach would disappear and a hollow, aching feeling would take its place.

Why, why, why had he come back? Nothing had gone right since that day at Penbury Manor when she had turned to see him standing on the path behind her. There had been no sign of him since he had walked away with Dimity at the Starbridge Hotel. Jane should have been glad, but somehow it was worse spending her whole time wondering if he was going to turn up and then feeling restless and irritable and unaccountably deflated when he didn't.

Absorbed in her thoughts, unaware of where she was going, Jane ended up at last at the edge of the woods, looking down on Penbury Manor. Quiet and tranquil, the old house seemed to glow in the afternoon sunshine, looking exactly as it had looked ten years ago when she had stood here with Lyall.

Jane looked around her with a sinking sense of recognition. What had brought her here, to the one part of the woods she had scrupulously avoided ever since that summer? This had been their place, hers and Lyall's. The clearing was overgrown now, but there was the log where they had sat and planned where they would go when they left Penbury, there was the tree that Lyall had kissed her against the very first time they had made love, and over there the place where he used to spread the blanket. Jane felt as if she was drowning in memories. She fought to stay afloat, but it was no good. She could practically feel the rough bark of the tree as she had leant against it, weak with desire, while Lyall had shaken out the rug, could still see him look up at her with that reckless, irresistible smile that had drawn her unresisting over towards him.

So vivid was the scene that when Lyall spoke her name from the edge of the clearing Jane wasn't even surprised to feel the breath dry in her throat. It seemed quite natural to see him there, part and parcel of the tug of time that had brought her here this afternoon. The memories had left her disorientated, disjointed, so that

all she could do was look back at him, her normally
steady grey eyes huge and dark.

In the shadowy light, Lyall looked overwhelmingly
distinct but the blue eyes were unreadable as he walked
across the clearing towards her. There was something
about his solidity that was both reassuring and un-
nerving, but he was undeniably real, and Jane drew a
ragged breath.

'How long have you been here?'

'Not long.'

The vibrancy and immediacy of his presence sent the
memories fading back into the past. Whenever Lyall was
there, it was impossible to be aware of anything but the
here and now, of the man he was and the way he made
her feel. 'What are you doing here?' she asked unsteadily.

'Just walking,' he said. 'And thinking.' He paused and
looked at Jane, poised warily as if for flight beneath the
old chestnut tree. 'What about you?'

'The same really,' said Jane a little lamely.

Lyall regarded her thoughtfully. 'It seems to me that
you're not nearly as busy as you pretend to be, Jane.
Long lunches with Alan, afternoon walks in the
woods...when do you have time to write those crisp
progress reports you send me so dutifully?'

'I could say the same for you,' she retorted, re-
covering her breath and hoping to hide her uncertainty
behind a show of belligerence. 'Don't you have a multinational company to run?'

The blue eyes lit with amusement. 'My company's well
under control, thank you, Jane.'

'You surprise me,' she said waspishly. 'I gathered from
what you said before that none of your staff could
function without you hanging over their shoulders.
Shouldn't you be annoying them instead of hanging
around here? For someone so keen to forget his roots,
you seem to spend an awful lot of time in Penbury!'

'I thought I wanted to forget my roots too,' admitted Lyall unexpectedly. 'But something keeps bringing me back.'

'I don't suppose that something could be a pair of big green eyes, could it?' snapped Jane before she could help herself.

He put his hands in his pockets and rocked back on his heels. 'You're not jealous by any chance, are you, Jane?'

'Certainly not,' she said coldly. 'Dimity's welcome to you! I'm just surprised that you should fall for all that gush and giggle, that's all!'

'That's good coming from a girl who's fallen for a man like Alan Good!' said Lyall with something of an edge. 'I wouldn't describe him as "gush and giggle", of course. More like stuff and starch, perhaps? Or pomposity and pretension?'

She glared at him. 'Alan is very nice.'

'So you keep saying.' He eyed her moodily. 'Is it true that you're going to marry him?' he asked abruptly, almost as if the question had been forced out of him.

Jane froze. 'Who told you that?'

'Dimity met him at the opening of some exhibition in the art gallery. Apparently they recognised each other from the hotel, and had a nice little chat together, all about how you and Alan were planning to get married.'

She knew just which exhibition it had been. Alan had asked her to go, but she hadn't wanted to face another evening trying to convince him that she meant what she said and had made some excuse instead. Her lips tightened. Alan had no business telling Dimity that they were engaged!

'And Dimity rushed straight back to you with the news, did she?' she asked with a chilly look, but Lyall only shrugged.

'Is it true?'

'Why so surprised?' she said. 'You were the one who was so keen for me to prove that I wasn't a coward about marriage. You were all for me taking the plunge, if you remember.'

He scowled. 'Only if you loved him.'

'What makes you think that I don't?'

'Because I saw you with him at lunch that day,' he said. 'You were grey with boredom, and I'm not surprised. You can say what you like about how *nice* he is, but the man's obviously a pompous prig, and you know it, Jane. You don't love him. You probably wish you did, but you don't.'

'I do!' she lied.

'No, you don't,' Lyall repeated inexorably. 'I'm prepared to bet that you only asked him out to lunch that day because I'd invited Dimity out.'

The nerve of the man was unbelievable! Jane was angry now, too angry to acknowledge that he was right. 'Do you really think I give a damn what you do, or who you do it with?' she demanded in a voice that shook with fury. 'I couldn't have cared less if you and Dimity had stripped off and conducted your own private orgy in the middle of the Starbridge Hotel!'

'Oh, I think you could, Jane,' said Lyall softly, and suddenly he was standing very close to her. 'I think you remember the past just as well as I do.'

'I don't,' she said, backing away until she came up against the tree.

'Yes, you do. There was always something between us then, and there's something between us now.'

'No.' She shook her head almost frantically. 'There's nothing now. *Nothing.*'

There was a strumming silence as wary grey eyes stared into relentless blue ones. Lyall didn't believe her, that was obvious. He knew she was lying.

'Do you remember this place, Jane?' he asked suddenly.

She looked away, to the place where they had first made love. Her heart was slamming painfully against her ribs and her throat felt tight and dry. 'No,' she lied again.

'I do,' he said. 'I remember it well. I'd arranged to meet you here and I was late. When I arrived, you were waiting for me. You were standing under this tree, just where you're standing now.' Jane made to move away, but he put out an iron hand and drew her back. 'You stood there and smiled at me,' he said.

'D-did I?'

'You were wearing jeans and a plain white shirt, and the sun was filtering through the leaves on to your face, just like it is now.' Lyall's voice was deep and slow, like a warm breath on her skin. 'I'd wanted to make love to you ever since I knocked you off your bike that day, but you'd been warned against me, hadn't you? You were a good girl, and good girls didn't have anything to do with the Hardings. I had to work hard for you, didn't I, Jane? You were a challenge, and I've never been able to resist a challenge. All the other girls I'd known had made too much effort. They were always overdressed or over-eager or both, but you were different. You were cool and beautiful, with the clearest, steadiest grey eyes I'd ever seen, and when you turned and smiled at me that day I knew you were mine.'

Jane's knees felt weak and she leant back against the tree. She could feel the rough bark at her back, and she dug her fingers into it as if for support. Lyall's voice was reverberating right through her, stirring old memories, rekindling old feelings. She wanted to shout at him, to push him away, but she was transfixed, bewitched by the past and by his nearness.

'Do you remember what happened next, Jane?' Lyall went on, his voice deeper and lower than ever, but the breath was strangled in her throat and all Jane could do was shake her head in a last attempt at denial.

'I think you do,' he said. 'I think you remember how everything fell into place that day. You knew that the time had come as well as I did. I didn't have to say anything. I came across to you and I stood right where I'm standing now. We just looked at each other, didn't we, Jane? And then, very slowly, I undid the buttons on your shirt.' Lyall lifted his hands as he spoke and began to unbutton Jane's pale blue shirt as slowly, as deliberately as he had done before.

Jane closed her eyes against the avalanche of remembered sensation. 'Don't do this to me, Lyall,' she whispered, but she didn't, couldn't, pull away, and Lyall simply carried on, tugging her shirt free of her trousers so that he could undo the last two buttons and drift his fingers down from her throat to cup her breasts. His hands were strong and sure, burning like fire as they explored the softness of her skin. Jane felt hollow with desire. The slow scorch of his touch snarled every nerve in her body and set a low ache of need thudding inside her.

Lyall rubbed his thumbs almost thoughtfully over her tingling nipples and felt Jane quiver. 'Do you remember now, Jane?' he asked, and slid his hands down to her waist to pull her unhurriedly against him. 'I could feel you trembling when I touched you and I knew that you wanted me as much as I wanted you.'

'No,' Jane managed with an immense effort. 'No.'

'Yes,' said Lyall, the implacability in his voice at odds with the tantalising feel of his fingers. He bent his head until barely a breath separated them. 'We both knew that we had been leading up to this moment ever since we met. It had all come to this one point when there were just the two of us beneath this tree and I kissed you... like this,' he finished softly, and his mouth came down on hers and all thought, all memory, dissolved into the old enchantment.

Jane was lost. She had been lost the moment he'd touched her, the moment she had seen him standing on the other side of the clearing. Desire rippled over her skin as Lyall kissed her, a long, deep, intoxicating kiss that swept her through time to a place where there was no past and no present, to a place where she and Lyall had always belonged together and where nothing mattered but the touch of his hands and the searing warmth of his mouth and the feel of his hard body pressing her back against the tree.

Adrift in enchantment, abandoned to spinning sensation, oblivious to the rough bark digging into her, Jane slid her arms around Lyall to pull him closer. Her hands spread over his back, savouring the warmth of his skin through his shirt and the steely feel of the muscles that flexed beneath her touch.

Lyall's grip on her tightened as she melted into his kiss so utterly that an electric excitement seared into life, scorching through the sweetness to invest their kisses with a new hunger and urgency. He lifted his head long enough to mutter Jane's name almost accusingly, before jerking her back against him, and after that they both lost control. They kissed desperately, frantic to hold each other tighter, closer, clinging together against the rocketing desire.

Jane arched her body beneath Lyall's insistent exploration. His hands were hard and demanding, sliding down her spine and curving possessively over her skin as his mouth left hers to press kisses down her throat to her breasts. The touch of his lips, of his tongue, sent need shafting through her with an intensity that was almost painful and she tipped her head back, gasping his name without thinking.

'Lyall!'

Slowly, excruciatingly slowly, he kissed his way back up to her lips. '*Now* do you remember, Jane?' he murmured raggedly against the corner of her mouth. 'Do you remember how it was that day? Do you remember what happened next?'

CHAPTER SEVEN

JANE'S hands fell from his shirt. 'I wanted to forget,' she said bitterly, appalled at how defenceless she had been against Lyall's kisses. Her grey eyes were dark and enormous in her white face and she pulled the sides of her shirt together with hands that shook uncontrollably.

'Why?' Lyall laid a hand against her cheek but Jane struck it away. 'Why try and deny what was between us all those years ago, what's still between us?'

Jane slumped back against the support of the tree and turned her face away. 'It was all over ten years ago,' she said despairingly, but it wasn't clear whether she was trying to convince herself or Lyall.

'It isn't over, Jane,' he said. 'I thought it was over too. When I first saw your name on the tender for Penbury Manor, I honestly thought you didn't mean anything to me any more. I thought that if I met you I'd be able to treat you just like anyone else, but then I came back, and saw you standing among the flowers with your arms full of roses and the sun on your hair, and I knew that nothing had changed. You were just the same.'

'I'm not the same.' She began to do up her shirt with fumbling fingers. She felt sick and dizzy, as if she had been dropped from a great height, but as the first shock of shame and humiliation faded welcome anger flickered through her. 'I'm not the same at all. I was a gullible little fool when you knew me before, but I've had to grow up since then. I began to grow up the day you left for London with Judith and I had to face everyone

knowing that they all knew what a fool I'd made of
myself over you.'

Lyall stepped away at that, and his face closed. 'You
could have come too. I asked you to come. I *begged* you
to come.'

'You didn't really expect me to join a cosy little
threesome with you and Judith, did you?'

'I tried to explain about Judith,' he said angrily. 'But
you wouldn't listen. I thought if I gave you a chance to
calm down after you'd seen us in the woods you'd think
about what we'd had together and realise that you'd got
it all wrong, but you didn't, did you? You weren't even
going to see me. I had to force my way past your father.'

How well Jane remembered that terrible day. The icy
hand of misery around her heart, the furious voices in
hall and then Lyall standing in the doorway, his face
tense with anger. He had really expected her to fall back
into his arms! 'Come away with me now, Jane,' he had
urged. 'Judith doesn't mean anything. We'll never have
a future in Penbury. It's too full of small-minded, mean-
spirited people. Things will be different in London.'

Now Lyall was looking down at her with exactly the
same expression of angry frustration. 'Did you mean
what you said then, Jane? That everything you'd told
me before was a lie? That you'd never had any intention
of leaving Penbury?'

'Why did you find it so hard to believe?' she asked
bravely.

'Because I remembered how clear your eyes had been
when you told me you loved me, and because I couldn't
believe that you were so pathetic that you'd give in to
your father and agree to stay stuck in Penbury for the
rest of your life.'

Jane tucked her shirt furiously back into her trousers.
'Has it never occurred to you, Lyall, that sometimes it
can take more courage to stay than to go?'

He snorted. 'Not in your case, Jane. You wouldn't come with me because you were a coward, and that's all there was to it!'

'Don't you dare call me a coward!' The surge of anger was wonderfully invigorating. Jane pushed her hair angrily behind her ears and faced Lyall, incandescent with rage. 'Do you have any idea what it's been like for me these last ten years? Do you have any idea of how humiliating it was to have to admit to everyone that they'd been right about you all along? I'd told them all that they didn't understand you, that you weren't like they all said, and then you took off with Judith, which just went to prove how much *I* knew about it! Still, at least I wasn't stupid enough to go with you,' she swept on. 'You used to go on about my father keeping me in Penbury, but it was you he objected to, not my going away—and how right he was! He was quite happy to let me go to horticultural college.'

'Not so happy that he let you finish the course,' Lyall put in sardonically.

'He didn't have a heart attack deliberately! I *had* to come home. He was so ill, and fretting about the firm only made him worse. I suppose if it had been your father you'd have just let him kill himself, but I couldn't do that. I gave up my course and I learnt to do the accounts and deal with suppliers and tender for work and do all the worrying instead of my father. I can't tell you how many nights I stayed at the office trying to balance the books, trying to find ways to cut costs, trying not to let Dad guess how bad things were. Do you think that was easy for me? Do you think it was easy to give up my dreams of a career in horticulture or to have to make men redundant, or scrape around to find the money to send Kit to university? Do you think it was easy to watch Dad die anyway?' Angry tears glittered in her eyes and

Jane dashed them away with the back of her hand. 'Well, do you, Lyall? *Do* you?'

She glared at Lyall, whose expression was still and unreadable. 'No,' he admitted at last.

'Then don't ever call me a coward again!' All the pent-up feelings of the last few weeks came spilling out now. Shaken to the core by her reaction to his kiss, Jane clung to the surging anger that blotted out the memory of how she had gasped with pleasure in his arms. 'You're the coward, Lyall! You like to talk about your freedom and your independence, don't you? But they're just another way of saying that you're too much of a coward ever to commit yourself to anybody. I was lucky to last three months! How long did Judith last—a month? two?—before you got bored and moved on to someone else, someone who wouldn't threaten your precious independence, someone desperate enough to accept you on your own terms, regardless of what she might feel or want? That doesn't matter to you, does it? All that matters is what *you* want!'

Lyall opened his mouth to interrupt, but she wouldn't listen. She didn't want to argue with him, she just wanted to *tell* him. 'I suppose it amused you to come back here and stir up old memories. You never stopped to think that I might not want to see you again, that I was perfectly happy as I was. Oh, no! You were bored and you wanted some fun, just like you were bored ten years ago and thought you'd see just how big a fool you could make of me. Now you're trying to do just the same thing, only this time I'm ten years older and I'm not prepared to let you trample all over my life like you did before! You're selfish and arrogant and irresponsible and I don't want anything to do with you, so will you please just go away and leave me and Penbury alone?'

Lyall's expression was stony, and he was very white about the mouth. 'Gladly,' he said tightly. 'I've got better things to do with my time than stand around being accused of selfishness by a girl who never once gave any thought to what *I* might have felt ten years ago. But then you never were really interested in me, were you, Jane? You were tired of being a good girl and you wanted to prove that you didn't always have to do what you were told. You were waiting for someone and it just happened to be me. I was your taste of excitement, your token rebellion, but you didn't like it for long. If you hadn't seen me with Judith that day, you'd have found some other excuse to run back to daddy.' He gave a mirthless laugh. 'And to think I thought you were mismatched with that prat Alan Good! You're perfect for each other! You can get stuck in a rut together and nothing will ever upset your nice, safe, blinkered view of the world. Well, you needn't worry, Jane,' he finished bitterly. 'Alan's welcome to you. You can keep him and Penbury. I don't want any more to do with either of you.'

'Good,' Jane shouted after him as he turned and strode away, but he didn't look back. 'Good,' she said again when he had gone, to reassure herself that she meant it, but she wrapped her arms about herself as if she was cold, and her voice echoed desolately in the silent, empty wood.

When Lyall rang the office the next day, she refused to talk to him. 'He says he only wants to apologise,' said Dorothy, who had buzzed her through the intercom and was trying desperately to disguise her curiosity.

'I don't care,' said Jane. 'I don't want to talk to him.'

She had said all she had to say to Lyall yesterday. A restless night reliving that shattering kiss over and over again and lashing herself for having kissed him back so hungrily had only hardened her resolve never to see him again. She would continue to send him progress reports as agreed in the contract, but there would be no need for her to discuss anything with him personally. The men were doing good work at the manor, and it was too late for him to change his mind about the first stage of the contract now. As for the later stages, well, she would just have to worry about that later, but for all Lyall's faults she didn't think that he was vindictive. He would probably just hand everything over to his company secretary anyway if he meant what he had said about not wanting any more to do with Penbury.

The thought should have made Jane happy, but instead she was tense and restless. Lyall's words nagged at her. Did he really believe that she had used him? He had accused her of being selfish and cowardly and dull. Was that really how he saw her? Was that how she *was*?

Jane didn't want to answer that. She threw herself into work instead, blitzing the pile in her in-tray, bringing the accounts up to date and clearing out the three filing cabinets that were so full she couldn't shut the drawers properly. The office was a lot better organised when she had finished, but nothing else had changed. Lyall's scathing opinion still echoed uncomfortably in her ears and, to make matters worse, Alan was still being persistent. He had taken to dropping round unexpectedly in the evenings, something he had never done before, and as a result Jane spent longer and longer hours in the office trying to avoid him. Lyall would have said that she had used Alan too, she thought guiltily. There was Kit to think about too. She knew that he would be waiting for her to send him some money, but the bank manager had turned down flat her request for a loan, which meant that she couldn't put off selling the house much longer. All in all, Jane had had enough of men.

Lyall didn't make it any easier for her to put him out of her mind by ringing every day. Every day Dorothy buzzed Jane and asked if she would speak to him, and every day Jane refused.

'Why won't you talk to him?' Dorothy was moved to remonstrate after this had been going on for a couple of weeks. 'He sounds so nice on the phone. I can hardly believe it's the same Lyall Harding.'

'Oh, it's the same Lyall all right,' said Jane bitterly.

'He used to be so wild when he was young.' Dorothy shook her head sadly. 'Poor boy, I don't think he can have been very happy. I knew his mother, you know. She was a beautiful girl, but she wasn't strong enough to stand up to Joe Harding. He was a very difficult man.' She sighed and shook her head again as she stuffed invoices into envelopes. 'I think he loved Mary in his own way, but he was so jealous of her, he made her life a misery. He used to bully Lyall too, until he was old enough to stand up for himself. I'm not surprised that Lyall went off the rails. He hated not being able to protect his mother, and making trouble was the only way he had of hitting back at his father. Not many people saw it like that, of course. All they saw was that he was leading their sons into trouble and breaking their daughters' hearts. I think they were all relieved when he ran away from home.'

Dorothy's hands had fallen still as she remembered. 'I saw Mary not long after he left. She looked terrible. Lyall was only just seventeen, and of course she was worried sick about him, but she told me she knew that if he'd stayed there would have been real trouble between him and his father. I think in a way he left for her, and he came back for her, too. She must have waited before she let him know how ill she was, and she nearly left it too late. Lyall only got back the day before she died.' Heaving a sigh, Dorothy shook herself and picked up another envelope. 'But of course, I don't need to tell you all this, do I, Jane? You must have known him better than anyone.'

Had she? Jane looked blindly down at the desk. She hadn't known about Lyall's unhappiness at home. She hadn't known that he had only come back to see his mother die. She hadn't known how he had really felt at all. 'You never were really interested in me', he had said, and he had been right. Preoccupied with her concerns for Kit and her uncharacteristic defiance of her father, she hadn't thought about what Lyall might be feeling. He had been so much older than she, had always seemed so strong, so vital, that it had never occurred to her that he might have problems of his own.

'I'm not sure that I did,' she told Dorothy slowly. 'He never talked about his parents. If he hated his father so much, why did he stay here after his mother died?'

'Joe went to pieces after Mary died,' Dorothy remembered. 'I suppose Lyall felt that he had to get him back on his feet again, in spite of everything, but that wouldn't have been the main reason why he stayed.'

'What was, then?'

Dorothy looked at Jane in disbelief. 'You, of course! You wouldn't have known him before, but he'd been away eight years and he'd changed a lot. Before he would run around with a different girl every week, but that summer there was only you.'

And Judith. And how many other girls he'd never told her about? Jane's face closed and she turned away. 'He hadn't changed that much,' she said, and thought of how he had flirted with Dimity. 'He still hasn't.'

She went into her office and tried to concentrate on the latest progress report, but Dorothy's words niggled at her. She *had* been self-centred, just as Lyall had said. True, she had been very young, but she could have made more of an effort to understand what had made him the man he was. It didn't change how she felt about him now, Jane reassured herself hastily, but if he rang again she would talk to him, not to say that she was sorry—

what did *she* have to apologise for?—but just to prove that she was capable of behaving in a cool, civilised way if he was.

But Lyall didn't ring. It seemed as if the message had finally got through, just as she had changed her mind. Jane told herself that it was all for the best, but perversely began to miss Dorothy telling her that Lyall was on the line. Every time the phone went she jumped, and if she'd been out she found herself flicking quickly through the messages Dorothy had left in case there was one from him.

Eventually, exasperated by her own contrariness and unable to bear the thought of another weekend snatching up the phone only to find Alan on the other end, Jane decided to take up a long-standing invitation to visit friends in Bristol. If Lyall didn't want to get in touch, that was fine!

When Alan heard about her proposed trip, he was all for going with her. 'We could visit my parents on the way back,' he said eagerly.

'No.' Jane took a deep breath and steeled herself to tell Alan once and for all that marriage was out of the question. By the time she had finished, he was looking like a dog that had been kicked and she felt terrible, but at least he seemed to have realised at last that she meant what she said.

'I'm sorry,' she finished a little inadequately, but she thought it was better to dash Alan's hopes now rather than later. 'I hope we can still be friends, though.'

Alan seemed to take that as an encouraging sign and perked up a little, but he couldn't shake her resolve to go away on her own, and it was with a sigh of relief that Jane got into the van that Friday afternoon. She was alone at last, and she wasn't going to think about Alan, Kit *or* Lyall all weekend!

She did, of course. It was good to see Beth and Tony again but even as she laughed and chatted part of her mind was drifting back to Penbury and wondering if her phone was ringing. Lyall could always leave a message on her answering machine, she reassured herself, before catching herself up irritably. What was the *matter* with her? She wasn't supposed to care whether he rang or not.

It didn't stop her rushing to the phone to see if there were any messages as soon as she got home, or feeling her heart drop when she realised that there weren't. She went out into the garden and vented her frustration on the weeds. So what if Lyall didn't want to talk to her any more? He had obviously given up on Penbury, just as he had said he would. It had been nearly a month since he had been down—not that she had been counting!—and he was no doubt busy pestering some other poor female. Whoever she was, she had Jane's sympathy!

Monday saw Jane driving grumpily up to the manor with a load of paint for Lyall's temporary quarters—not that it looked as if he was going to be using them. Still, the contract said decorate the rooms, so decorate them they would.

Dimity was getting out of her car when Jane drove up. 'Hiya, Jane!' she gushed. '*Great* to see you!' Her effusiveness set Jane's teeth on edge and rang warning bells in her mind. Why was Dimity suddenly being her best friend? She was the kind of girl who usually only bothered when there were men around to impress with her sweetness. 'How was your weekend?'

'Fine,' said Jane shortly, obliged out of common civility to ask in return how Dimity's had been.

'Oh, it was *wonderful*!'

Why couldn't she talk like anyone else, instead of stressing every other word in that gratingly sweet, breathy voice? Jane bared her teeth in a brief smile and turned to start unloading the paint out of the back of the van, but Dimity was undeterred by her lack of enthusiasm.

'Lyall came down for the weekend, you know,' she confided, with a coy look, then squeaked as one of the paint cans crashed to the ground, narrowly missing her foot. 'Careful!'

'Sorry,' said Jane, wishing it had hit her.

Dimity pushed her artfully tumbled curls away from her face. 'Where was I? Oh, yes, Lyall...he's *so* nice, isn't he?'

'He can be very charming when he wants to be.' Jane concentrated fiercely on unloading the paint.

'He's always charming to *me*.' Dimity opened her eyes wide and sighed nostalgically. 'This weekend was the first chance we've had to really *talk*. Do you know that feeling when you meet a man and everything's so *right* you feel as if you've known each other for years?'

'No,' said Jane, but she might as well have spared her breath.

'It was like that for Lyall and me,' said Dimity with a smug look. 'Of course, Lyall's known a lot of women in the past, but, judging by the things he was saying, I really think he's ready to change and settle down.'

'Really?' said Jane coldly, wondering if Lyall had lumped her in with all those other women he had known or whether Dimity was just guessing.

Dimity twisted a curl around one finger and simpered. 'Oh, yes; in fact he's even... But I'd better not say any more.' She cast a triumphant glance at Jane. 'I think he doesn't want anyone but me to know his plans just yet.'

'In that case you'd better not go around gossiping about them, had you?'

The pretty face tightened at Jane's reproof, but it would take more than that to make Dimity lose her honeyed sweetness. 'Lyall and I saw Alan in the pub on Saturday,' she went on, changing tack. 'The poor man was looking rather down because you'd gone off for the weekend without him, but I managed to cheer him up,' she remembered, with another complacent glance at Jane whom she obviously pitied for her inability to handle men. 'You'll have to be careful you don't lose him,' she added playfully. 'Gorgeous men like Alan don't grow on trees, you know.' And, having proffered her bit of sisterly advice, she wafted off into the manor without even offering to carry one of the paint cans.

Jane looked after her with dislike. What did she mean about Lyall changing his plans? And if Dimity really thought her simpering silliness was enough to make a man like Lyall settle down, she was even more of a fool than Jane had thought!

But who was she to talk of fools when she had spent the whole weekend wondering if he had rung her? With a sigh, Jane picked up the first two cans of paint and trudged towards the manor.

The phone was ringing when she got back to the office, and Dorothy picked it up as she smiled a welcome. 'Oh, hello,' she said into the receiver, bridling with pleasure. 'How nice to hear from you... I'm fine... No, not really... She's working much too hard as usual... That's *exactly* what I say...' There was a long pause and then Dorothy began scribbling down notes. 'Yes... yes... yes... yes, I've got that.'

'Who is it?' Jane whispered, and Dorothy covered the mouthpiece with her hand.

'Lyall Harding.'

Jane's knees felt suddenly weak. 'Oh. Well, I'll be in my office,' she said with studied casualness. Settling at her desk, she composed herself as she waited for Dorothy to buzz her. She would speak to him, just this once, to tell him that she was absolutely fine, in spite of Dorothy's heavy hints, and that she wasn't in the least bothered to hear that he was thinking of settling down with Dimity.

She waited, but there was no buzz. Instead there was a tell-tale 'ping' as Dorothy put down the receiver, and then the clicking sound of the keyboard as she resumed her typing.

Jane frowned and went through to the other room. 'Didn't he want to talk to me?' she demanded, more than a little piqued.

'He said he knew there wasn't any point in me asking you if you wanted to speak to him,' said Dorothy apologetically. 'So he just gave me a message.'

'Oh.' Jane knew that she was behaving illogically, but it didn't make her feel any less disgruntled. Lyall could have insisted on Dorothy trying to put him through, couldn't he? 'Well, what was it?'

'Apparently you mentioned fireplaces in one of your progress reports? For the guest bedrooms?' Dorothy peered at her notes. 'Anyway, he said he's just come across a supply of exactly the right type somewhere in east London, but he needs someone to go and pick them up tomorrow or he'll lose the deal. He thought you could send a couple of the men in one of the vans.'

'Tomorrow's Tuesday,' said Jane, twisting the desk diary round to check. 'It's all very well to ring up in a grand way and order someone down to London, but they're all so busy at the moment. Colin's off sick, and Jim's wife is expecting a baby any minute now, so he can't go. Ray's doing a job for Mrs Fothergill... I suppose I could pull someone off the manor, but we're on a tight enough schedule as it is.' She tapped her pen against her teeth. 'Did Lyall say exactly where this place is?'

'Just the East End. He said he would be out in the morning, but if whoever you send calls in at his office and asks for his secretary she'll be able to give them precise directions.'

Jane considered. 'If Lyall's not going to be there anyway, I might as well go myself,' she decided. 'I haven't got any appointments tomorrow, and there's bound to be someone to help with the loading. I can take the big van and be back here tomorrow evening.'

'It's a long drive on your own,' said Dorothy doubtfully, but Jane scoffed at her, suddenly enthused by the prospect of a day out of the office doing something different.

'Nonsense! It shouldn't take more than a couple of hours to get there at the most.'

In the event, it took her nearly four, thanks to roadworks on the M4 and an accident blocking the exit from the motorway. She had reckoned without crossing London, too, and by the time she reached the City Jane was feeling distinctly frazzled. As she tried to turn down yet another one-way street, she wished she had stayed at home with the dull old routine that Lyall thought she liked so much.

Why couldn't he have his headquarters somewhere more accessible? It was a nightmare trying to find her way through the maze of streets in the big van, particularly when everyone else seemed to know exactly where they were going and tooted impatiently whenever she hesitated.

Her temper was not improved when she eventually found Multiplex and discovered that the car park was full. Typical, thought Jane crossly, driving round again. The only space where she could possibly park the van was marked 'Reserved for Chairman', but since that was Lyall and she was here on his orders there was no reason why she shouldn't park there, she reasoned. It was only for five minutes, after all, while she went in to get directions.

Encouraged by the fact that Lyall was obviously still out, Jane parked the van at a jaunty angle and headed around to the front entrance. Close to, the Multiplex headquarters was a dauntingly modern building, strikingly designed in glass and gleaming tiles, and about as different from Penbury Manor as could be imagined.

She slunk up to the reception desk, feeling uncomfortably out of place in her jeans and faded blue shirt. They might be practical for loading fireplaces, but they made her look horribly shabby compared to the immaculate suits the receptionists were wearing.

Lyall's assistant would be down in just a moment, she was told. In the meantime, perhaps she would like to take a seat? The receptionist gestured over to some comfortable-looking chairs around a small pool where the soaring lines of the lobby were softened by lush green plants. Automatically, Jane pressed her thumb into their pots to feel the soil and checked the undersides of some leaves, but they all seemed to be thriving. Lyall probably kept an eye on the person looking after the plants too.

Lyall. Was it possible that the wild young man she had first known had risen to own all of this? Jane perched gingerly on the edge of a leather sofa and watched the buzz of activity in the hall. These men in their sharp suits, these smart, beautifully dressed women were all answerable to him in one way or another.

As if her thoughts had conjured him up out of thin air, the automatic doors opened and Lyall strode in, accompanied by four other men. Immediately the atmosphere changed. The receptionists perked up visibly and everyone else in hall seemed somehow to straighten. There was no question that Lyall was the focus of all attention. His power was obvious in the way he stood, effortlessly drawing the eye although he was dressed exactly like his companions in a well-cut suit and tie.

Even at a distance, Jane was aware of the deference with which the other men treated him.

She had grabbed a newspaper to hide behind as soon as she saw him, and peered round it as the group waited by the lift. She saw Lyall shake hands with two of the men as the doors slid open, and ducked hurriedly back behind her paper. What if that was his secretary coming down in the lift? She might tell him that Jane was here, and she wouldn't put it past Lyall to think that she had come chasing up to London just in the hope of seeing him.

The next moment a hand pushed down the paper in front of her face, and Jane found herself staring up into a pair of familiar dark blue eyes. Their expression was less familiar, a cool, guarded look almost masking the blaze of recognition.

'I didn't know you could read upside-down, Jane!'

Jane looked at the paper. Sure enough, she was holding it the wrong way up. Flushing, she dropped it on to the seat beside her. 'I thought you were supposed to be out,' she said truculently, flustered by his nearness and the memory of the last time they had met when they had kissed so passionately and argued so bitterly. Seeing him here, surrounded by the evidence of his power and authority, made her unsure of herself.

'I've been out all morning,' said Lyall in a cool voice. 'I thought the van would have arrived long ago, which is why I left the instructions with my PA.' A frown creased his brow. 'Why are you here, anyway? I told Dorothy to get you to send a couple of your men.'

'I make the decisions in my company, not you,' Jane reminded him haughtily. 'And I decided that I could best be spared.'

'You look tired,' said Lyall bluntly. 'Dorothy said you'd been working too hard. The last thing you should be doing is flogging up and down the motorway in the rush-hour traffic.'

'You should have thought of that before you rang up issuing orders,' snapped Jane. 'And I'd appreciate it if you didn't discuss me with my secretary. There's nothing wrong with me. If I look tired, it's because I was held up on the motorway and then had to spend hours looking for your rotten office!'

'You should have listened to my advice and sent someone else,' he said unsympathetically. 'But then you never were very good at listening, were you, Jane?'

Their eyes met in a twanging moment of tension that excluded the rest of the thronging reception area, and then Lyall gave an explosive sigh that was half resignation, half exasperation. 'Well, since you're here, you'd better come up to my office and get the instructions.'

'Thank you, but there's no need for you to bother,' said Jane frigidly. 'Apparently your assistant is on her way down with them right now.'

Something flickered in Lyall's eyes. 'Is she, now?' he said, and turned to look towards the lifts, where an elegant woman in a grey skirt and a cream silk top had just stepped out and was looking around her. 'In fact, here she is now.' He lifted a hand.

Smiling an acknowledgement, his assistant glided over towards them. She seemed so poised that, without quite knowing why, Jane stood up.

'I'll leave you in her capable hands,' Lyall said, and with an indifferent nod he strode off towards the lifts, pausing only for a brief word with his secretary who seemed to hesitate and then nodded before crossing to Jane.

'Hello, Jane,' she said.

Biting her lip at the way Lyall hadn't even bothered to say goodbye, Jane didn't at first take in the other woman's appearance, but at the sound of her voice something clicked and she stared, hardly able to believe her eyes.

It was Judith.

CHAPTER EIGHT

'YOU probably don't remember me,' said Judith, misinterpreting Jane's blank expression.

'Yes...yes, I do.' Jane's head was whirling. Judith was the last person she had expected to see here. Could she really be Lyall's assistant? Why hadn't he told her, warned her? 'Y-you've changed,' she stammered. If Judith herself hadn't said anything, it was doubtful whether she would have recognised the truculent, aggressively crude girl in this poised, sophisticated woman. The auburn hair had been dyed jet-black then, the mouth twisted into a sneer instead of a composed smile.

'I hope so,' said Judith quietly. 'If I have, it's all thanks to Lyall. I owe everything to him.'

Jane was still struggling to adjust to the transformation. 'Lyall didn't tell me you were his assistant,' she managed at last, wondering if that was all Judith was.

'I get the impression that there's rather a lot Lyall hasn't told you,' said Judith. She glanced over her shoulder to see if Lyall had gone, and seemed to make up her mind about something. 'Look, shall we sit down? Lyall doesn't want me to get involved, but I think you should know the truth about what happened that summer, and he's too stiff-necked to tell you himself.' Sitting down on one of the sofas, she patted the seat beside her, and after a moment Jane followed her.

'What do you mean, the *truth*?' she asked slowly.

'There was never anything between Lyall and me, Jane. We were friends, but that's all. Honestly.'

Jane sat stiffly, grey eyes guarded. 'You looked like more than friends when I saw you together.'

'If only you hadn't seen us that day!' sighed Judith. 'I was in a terrible state about...something, and Lyall was comforting me—that's really all it was.' She saw that Jane was looking unconvinced and tried to explain again. 'We were at school together. Lyall was a couple of years older than me, but we used to raise hell together. We understood each other. Lyall's father was a bully, and his mother had had all the spirit crushed out of her, and neither of them seemed to care very much what Lyall did. As for me...' Judith paused, her eyes shadowed with memories. 'Well, let's just say that my parents would never have won any prizes for being caring or understanding either. Lyall took off as soon as he could, and by the time he came home—the time you met him— I was really off the rails. You name it, I'd done it, and the more people pointed their fingers at me, the more determined I became to live up to my reputation. Lyall was the only one who saw me for what I really was—a desperate, frightened little girl!'

Jane stared down at her hands, ashamed. She too had known Judith's reputation and had never stopped to wonder why she behaved so aggressively. Lifting her eyes, she looked directly at Judith. 'I'm sorry,' she said, conscious of how inadequate it sounded.

Judith waved her apology aside. 'I didn't make it easy for anyone to help me,' she acknowledged. 'Lyall was pretty much preoccupied with you that summer but he noticed that I was upset about something. He used to come and see me, and we'd talk. He was the only person who treated me like a human being at that time,' she added with a touch of bitterness. 'I wouldn't tell him what was wrong at first, but I didn't have anyone else to confide in.' She sighed at the memory. 'I was pregnant. To tell you the truth, I didn't know who the father was, and I didn't care, but I'd realised that suddenly everything had changed. I desperately wanted to keep the baby, but I didn't want it to grow up the way I had done, and I knew what would happen if my father found out.'

She glanced at Jane, who was twisting a ring around her finger. She was looking at the glossy green leaves of a rubber plant, but it was obvious that she was listening. 'The day you saw us in the woods, Lyall had just managed to get the truth out of me,' Judith went on. 'I was all mouth in those days, but the truth was that I didn't have a clue about how I could cope with a baby, and I was in a terrible state. After I'd told him how much I wanted to keep the baby, I just burst into tears, but he was wonderful. He put his arms around me and let me cry all over him. And then you arrived.'

There was a silence. For Jane the scene was as vivid as if it had only taken place that morning. Breathless in her haste to find Lyall and let him reassure her that everything her father had told her about him and Judith was a lie, she had burst into the clearing, but all she had seen was the two dark heads so close together, Lyall's arms around another girl, holding her close. Had it really just been for comfort?

'Lyall ran after you, of course,' Judith went on when Jane didn't say anything, 'but when he came back he said that you hadn't given him a chance to explain. He went to see you the next day, too, and when you told him that it was all over he came straight round to me. He said that he'd had enough of Penbury and that he was leaving, and that if I wanted I could go with him and he'd make sure I was all right.' She hesitated. 'I've never seen him look like that, before or since. I don't think he realised until then quite how much you meant to him. I did try to suggest that he talk to you again, but he wouldn't. He was too proud to admit how hurt he was. All he would say was that he was going, and that I wouldn't get another chance. So I took it,' she said simply. 'We left two days later.'

She looked at Jane again, and then at the pool. 'I honestly think it helped him to have someone else to look after, so that he didn't think too much about you. He was marvellous. When we first arrived in London, it was Lyall who sorted everything out. He found me somewhere to live and made sure I could look after the baby. He even found me a job, and when he came back from the States and Multiplex took off I joined as his assistant. I only work part-time so that I can look after Jonathan, my son, but having a job has given me my self-respect over the years, and he's a good man to work for, as well as the best friend anyone could ever have.'

Jane could hear the restful sound of water from the fountain, and the murmur of voices in the background, but everything seemed very distant. She moistened her lips. Why had she refused to listen when Lyall had tried to explain all this to her? Was it because she had been as pigheaded and prejudiced as he had said?

'I wish I'd listened to Lyall in the first place,' she said with difficulty. 'He said I was too cowardly to trust in him, and it looks as if he was right.'

'You were very young,' said Judith consolingly. 'I'd have been just as suspicious in your place. Lyall was— what? Twenty-five? Old enough to realise how hurt you were, anyway. But you know how stubborn he is!'

'You know him much better than I do,' said Jane sadly. She drew a deep breath. There was one more thing she needed to know. 'Did you ever . . . were you ever . . . ?'

'Lovers? No.' Judith shook her head with a tiny smile. 'I'm not saying I wouldn't have been willing at times, but at first I was obsessed with Jonathan, and after you Lyall was determined not to get involved like that with a woman again. He stuck to girls who knew the rules of the game and weren't interested in any kind of commitment. No, we were just friends, Jane, and we still are. I got married six years ago, and Lyall is just happy that *I'm* happy at last.' She paused, and then looked directly at Jane. 'I just wish that he could be as happy.'

There was another long silence. Jane looked at the water and thought of the way she had misjudged Lyall, of the years she had wasted in needless bitterness. She had accused Lyall of never thinking about anyone but himself. She had called him selfish, arrogant and irresponsible, but she hadn't given him the chance to tell her what a good friend he had been to Judith. She felt very small.

'Thank you for telling me,' she said at last. 'I didn't know.'

'I didn't think you did, and I thought you should, in spite of what Lyall says.'

'Yes.' Jane met Judith's gaze, her own very clear and direct. 'I'm sorry I misjudged you, Judith.'

The older woman smiled. 'Don't be. Everything's worked out happily for me. If you want to be sorry, tell Lyall,' she added, and Jane nodded slowly.

'I will.'

The last receptionists were getting ready to go home by the time Jane got back to the Multiplex headquarters after picking up the fireplaces, and the car park was emptying. She asked to speak to Judith, and took the lift up to the twelfth floor.

'Lyall's in a meeting,' said Judith, meeting her at the lift. 'I'm not sure how long he'll be, and I haven't had a chance to tell him that you're here. Are you sure you want to talk to him tonight?'

'Yes.' Jane had spent the last few hours remembering all the things she had said to Lyall, and it seemed desperately important to apologise as soon as she could. All she wanted to do was say that she was sorry, and then she would go. 'I don't mind waiting.'

Judith glanced at her watch and came to a decision. 'I've got to go and pick up Jonathan. Why don't you wait in my office? That way you'll be able to hear when the meeting's over.'

It was nearly seven o'clock when Jane heard the outer door of Lyall's office open. There was a murmur of farewells and promises to keep in touch, and then the sound of the door closing once more.

Jane stood up, smoothing her hands down her jeans. She wished she had something pretty and feminine to wear, even a dash of lipstick to give her Dutch courage, but she hadn't expected to need anything when she'd left home that morning to collect the fireplaces. Lyall knew exactly what she was like, anyway. Knocking quietly at the door, she pushed it open.

Lyall was sitting at a vast desk, tapping something into a computer. His jacket hung on the back of his chair and he had loosened his tie, but he still managed to look crisp and authoritative. Jane was initially taken aback to see that he wore horn-rimmed glasses, and he was frowning through them at the screen.

Absorbed in what he was doing, he didn't look up at first. 'You still here, Judith?' he asked absently. 'I thought you'd have gone hours ago.'

'It's not Judith,' said Jane. 'It's me.'

At the sound of her voice, Lyall's head jerked to see her hesitating nervously in the doorway, and he seemed to clamp down savagely on the blaze of expression in his face as he took off his glasses and got very slowly to his feet.

'Jane?' he said warily, almost as if he didn't trust his eyes.

'Yes.' Jane didn't seem to be able to say anything else. The fine speeches she had prepared on the long drive back from collecting the fireplaces had vanished from her mind like last night's dreams, and the more she grasped for them, the more elusive they became.

'Didn't you get the fireplaces?'

'Yes,' she said again.

'Then what are you doing here?'

Jane looked across at him from the door and drew a steadying breath. 'I came to say that I was sorry for the things I said last time we met. Judith told me what really happened that summer.'

'I told her not to!' Hunching his shoulders, Lyall turned away to the window and stood with his back to her, hands thrust ferociously into his pockets.

'Why?'

'Quite frankly, I didn't think it was worth it,' he said heavily. 'You'd made it crystal-clear that you didn't want anything more to do with me, and I didn't want Judith to get the same treatment. She finds it hard enough to talk about that period of her life as it is.'

'I'm glad she did tell me,' said Jane in a quiet voice. 'I just wish I'd met her before. I wish I'd listened to you when you tried to explain ten years ago. I wish...' She trailed off. Lyall's back told her nothing. She didn't even know if he was listening. 'Oh, it doesn't matter,' she said hopelessly. 'I just wanted to say that I was sorry, and that I was wrong to say that you never cared about anyone else. You obviously cared a lot about Judith, but I was too priggish to understand what it took to be a real friend.'

Her words seemed to fall into a pool of silence. Lyall still hadn't moved, and Jane shifted uneasily. 'Well, that was it, really,' she said awkwardly, and began to edge back towards the door. 'I'll go now.'

Lyall turned at that. 'Where are you going?'

'Back to Penbury.'

'Now?' He was frowning and his voice was sharp with irritation.

'Why not?'

'Because you're exhausted, that's why.'

Suddenly he was shrugging on his jacket, banging a key to exit from the computer, shoving papers into his briefcase. Thrown by the abrupt change from intimidating silence to brusque activity, Jane watched him with a perplexed expression.

'I'm fine,' she said, even though the mere thought of getting back into the van again and driving across London and through the chaos on the motorway made her head ache.

'You're not fine,' Lyall contradicted her flatly as he shuffled through files to pull out three or four and toss them into his briefcase as well. 'Those dark circles under your eyes make you look like a panda.'

'Thanks!'

'You've been driving all day,' he went on, ignoring her. 'It's stupid to flog back down the motorway when you're that tired.'

'I can't afford to stay in a hotel,' said Jane, still confused. She had been prepared for him to refuse to listen to her, to be angry or unforgiving, but she hadn't expected this irritable inquisition into her travel plans!

Lyall snapped his briefcase shut. 'I'm not suggesting you stay in a hotel,' he said. 'You can come and stay with me.'

'Oh, well, I don't think... I mean, I'm not sure——' she began, but he cut off her stammered protests.

'There's no need to panic!' he said curtly. 'I haven't got an elaborate seduction scene in mind, if that's what you're worried about. I'm flying to Frankfurt first thing tomorrow morning, and will have to leave at five o'clock, so I'm certainly not planning a late night.'

Jane stared at him, unsure of how to react. Lyall was behaving very oddly. One minute he wasn't even listening to her, and the next he was crossly insisting that she stay the night with him. Something of her confusion must have shown in her face, for Lyall blew out an abrupt breath and came round the desk towards her.

'Look, I'm sorry,' he said more evenly. 'I know how much it must have cost you to come here and apologise. I wasn't expecting to see you again, and I'd even succeeded in convincing myself that that was what I wanted, so I didn't feel like going through it all again. But now that you're here, and we can both admit that we made mistakes, do you think we can finally put the past behind us? Right now you're tired, I'm tired. We could both do with a quiet drink and a good meal and an early night. Or would you really rather spend the next three hours sitting in a traffic jam on the motorway?'

'What about the fireplaces?' said Jane feebly.

'There's a security guard in the car park here all night. The van'll be quite safe, and you can pick it up in the morning.'

'Well...'

'You can have one of the guest rooms,' Lyall promised, and held up crossed fingers, the old, familiar, irresistible smile glimmering in his eyes. 'Scout's honour!'

'I haven't got anything with me,' she said, weakening. Really, she was pathetic! There she had been, determined to say her piece and then retire with dignity, and all it took was the gleam in his eyes to cut the pride out from beneath her feet. Lyall knew it, too, for he simply smiled and took her arm, propelling her, unresisting, towards the door.

'You won't need anything,' he said. 'It's only me.'

Almost everyone else had gone, and the building hummed emptily as they walked down the corridor to the lifts. Lyall had dropped his hand from her arm as soon as they'd reached the door, but Jane's skin still tingled where his touch had burned through the cotton of her shirt. The lift slid downwards in silence. She didn't look at Lyall, but she was very aware of his massive strength and the easy way he stood.

He seemed content to be silent, with only a brief word to his chauffeur as they got into the car that was waiting outside the entrance. Jane sat back in the seat next to him, cocooned from the ceaseless London traffic by the car's luxury. She studied Lyall under her lashes. He *did* look tired. He had leant his head back and closed his eyes briefly, and she thought there was a drawn look around his mouth and eyes that she had never seen before. For the first time she noticed a few stray grey hairs at his temples, and her heart wrenched with sudden insight.

This was the real Lyall, a man with everyday cares and concerns, a man who had had a tiring day and just wanted a quiet evening at home. She had carried his image for so long in her mind that when he had reappeared she had reacted to him exactly as if he were the same reckless, dangerous young man she had loved all those years ago. She had looked no further than the lurking smile in his eyes, but it was she who was the same, not Lyall. Deep down, she was still the naïve young girl, cast into confusion by the merest touch of his hand, still too bound up with her own preoccupations to notice that he had changed, matured, and left her far behind.

Without warning, Lyall opened his eyes and caught her staring at him as if she had never seen him before, her own eyes grey and clouded with despair at lost opportunities. He didn't say anything, but the long look they exchanged said more than words ever could. Jane felt all the doubts and misunderstandings, all the accusations and bitter words, dissolve like mist in the sunshine, until all that was left in her heart was the shining knowledge that she loved him, that she always had, and always would.

Then Lyall looked away and made some comment to the chauffeur about the traffic. Jane felt curiously disembodied, suspended from reality, and the men's deep voices seemed to come from a long way away. Her pulse had started to beat with slow, thumping insistence and there was a trembling feeling deep inside her.

Careful, Jane, she warned herself. Don't spoil things now. They had only just reached a truce; it was too early to think about starting again. A drink, a meal, an early night in separate beds; that was all he had offered.

Lyall lived in a spectacular penthouse flat in Belgravia. It had wide, sliding doors leading out on to a roof terrace with a view over the square. There was a pub on the far side, half hidden behind the trees, and people were sitting and standing outside, enjoying the warm summer night, their laughter drifting up across the square to where Jane stood with her hands on the smooth balustrade.

'Here you are.' Lyall appeared through the glass doors and handed her a glass of wine. 'Let's sit down.'

Jane felt ridiculously shy as they sat side by side, not touching, on a carved bench set among exuberant container plants. She broke off a sprig of rosemary and rubbed it between her fingers while she tried to think of something to say.

In the end it was Lyall who spoke first. 'You look tired,' he said abruptly, almost accusingly, as he had before. 'Haven't you been sleeping?'

'Of course I have,' Jane began instinctively, and then stopped. What was the point of denying it? 'Not very well,' she admitted.

'Why not?'

Jane lifted the rosemary and breathed in its fragrance. She didn't want to lie, but nor did she want to spoil the truce by telling him how many times she had lain awake thinking about that last argument and wishing that things had been different. 'There seems to have been a lot to think about recently,' she said unexpansively.

Lyall frowned. 'I thought winning the contract for Penbury Manor was going to be the end of your difficulties? It's certainly all going well as far as I'm concerned. Makepeace and Son is doing an excellent job. There aren't any problems, are there?'

'I'm not worried about work,' Jane said hastily.

'Then what?'

'Oh...' She gestured hopelessly. 'Things. Kit mostly.' It was the truth, if not the whole truth.

'I thought it might be Kit,' said Lyall, resigned. 'When *weren't* you worrying about Kit?'

Jane gave a wry smile. 'Kit's got someone else to worry about him now. He doesn't need me any more. He's just got married and is wildly happy in Buenos Aires.'

'Is he, now?' Lyall raised his brows. 'So what's the problem?'

'He needs some money. Dad left the firm to Kit and me jointly, and I know that he would have wanted Kit to have a lump sum when he got married, but things have been so tough over the last couple of years that I haven't got any capital set aside for emergencies.' She dropped the sprig of rosemary back into the pot. 'I went to see the bank manager, but he wasn't very encouraging, and the best he could suggest was that I sell the house, but with the market the way it is at the moment that might take ages.'

Lyall stared at her with a mixture of incredulity and exasperation. 'Do you really mean to tell me that you'd be prepared to sell the only home you've ever known just for that feckless brother of yours?'

'I don't want to,' sighed Jane. 'But I don't see what else I can do.'

'You could tell him that he'll have to wait for his money, for a start! Or—better still—earn it for himself.'

'I can't do that.'

'Why not?' he insisted.

Jane turned her face away and looked out across the
trees in the square to the distant rooftops. 'Because I
remember his face when our mother died,' she said in a
low voice, knowing that Lyall would never understand.
'He was only five, just a little boy.'

'And you were just a little girl,' said Lyall, as she had
known he would. 'What were you? Ten? Eleven? You
gave up your childhood for Kit, Jane. Don't give up your
home too. Kit's not a little boy any longer, and he's old
enough to look after himself.'

He was right, of course, but Jane knew that she would
never be capable of telling Kit that he couldn't rely on
her any longer. He was her brother, and as far as she
was concerned that meant that he could always depend
on her, no matter how old he was. She was silent,
thinking about Kit and how much she would hate to sell
Pear Tree Cottage.

Lyall was watching her averted face. 'There is another
alternative,' he said after a while, and she turned back
to him, hope lightening her grey eyes to silver.

'What?'

'I could lend you the money.'

The hope died as suddenly as it had flared. 'No,' she
said and shook her head. 'I wouldn't ask that of you.'

'You're not asking,' he pointed out. 'I'm offering.'

'Even so.' Jane shook her head again with finality. 'I
couldn't.'

'Think of it as an advance, if that makes it any easier,'
Lyall persisted.

She looked cautious. 'An advance?'

'Why not?' he asked reasonably. 'The contract says
that Multiplex will pay you on satisfactory completion
of the first stage of the work, but there's no reason why

we shouldn't advance you part of that for the work you've already done. It's money you've earned after all.'

'I don't know...' said Jane doubtfully, and it was Lyall's turn to shake his head, this time in mock-exasperation.

'Don't be so stiff-necked, Jane!' he said. 'It's not as if it's any skin off my nose. I'd have thought you would have approved of such an obviously sensible solution—or are you going to tell me that you're not as sensible as you used to be?'

'Of course I am!' she said automatically, and his smile tugged at the edge of her vision.

'In that case,' he said, 'all you need to do is smile and say thank you nicely.'

Jane wavered, then succumbed to his smile, just as she always had done, just as he had known that she would. 'Thank you nicely,' she said, and, turning to face him directly, she smiled.

Below, life continued to revolve noisily in the square. The evening air was full of the sounds of birds and voices and bursts of music punctuating the distant murmur of traffic, but up on the roof terrace it was very quiet. Jane could smell the rosemary on her fingers and the glass felt cool and smooth and heavy in her hand. Lyall's eyes were blue and warm as he smiled back at her, not the teasing, taunting smile that so unsettled her, but something more intense, something that set her heart pounding the way it had done in the car when she had looked at him and known that she loved him.

She felt her senses uncurl and open out until every inch of her quivered with awareness. Her toes tingled and her hair fell softly against her cheek, and she could feel the golden glow of the sun washing over her and through her.

The feeling stayed with her as she followed Lyall into the kitchen where he inspected the fridge and decided

that he could make her an omelette. Jane, who had expected him to whisk something from the freezer to the
microwave, was impressed by the competent way he
cracked eggs into a bowl and swirled butter round the
pan.

'I didn't know you could cook,' she said, slicing tom-
atoes for a salad. How much else was there about Lyall
that she didn't know?

'This is about as much as I can manage,' he con-
fessed. 'My housekeeper usually leaves me something,
but she's on holiday at the moment. To tell you the truth,
I tend to go out to eat when she's away, but it's only for
tonight and then I'm going away myself.'

'Where did you say you were going?'

'I've got a breakfast meeting at Frankfurt airport, then
I'm flying straight on to Japan. We've been working
round the clock to set up a major deal with the Japanese,
and we should be able to sign when I'm there. It's an
important development for Multiplex—almost as important as the Penbury Manor contract was for
Makepeace and Son!'

Jane smiled ruefully. 'I hope you've handled it better
than I did!'

Lyall grinned. 'Let's just say that negotiating with the
Japanese is very dull compared to doing business with
you!'

They ate the omelettes in the kitchen, and afterwards
Lyall found some fat black grapes and they shared them
together with what was left of a piece of Brie so ripe
that it oozed over the plate. Jane had forgotten how easy
Lyall could be to talk to, how easily he could make her
laugh. They made a tacit decision not to mention the
past or the love that they had once shared, but it lay
between them like a tangible thing all the same, silent
but impossible to ignore.

Lyall made some coffee and they took it into the sitting-room where the sliding doors were still thrown open to the night. Outside the sky was a deep violet-blue above the glow of the city lights. The traffic was still growling along Knightsbridge and across the square the noise from the pub had grown more raucous.

They sat at either end of a long sofa. Lyall had switched on a table lamp and its soft glow blurred the darkness as the easy atmosphere they had built so carefully trickled slowly but surely away and left in its place a slow, smouldering tension. Lyall was nowhere near her and his features were lost in the shadows, but Jane was acutely conscious of him in a way she hadn't been under the bright kitchen lights. Feelings crowded in on her, deep, dangerous feelings that strummed over her skin and whispered insidiously along her veins.

A drink, a quiet meal, a separate bed. That was all he had offered, she reminded herself feverishly as she blew on her coffee to cool it. If only she could cool herself as easily!

The air was vibrating with tension. Jane could feel it looping remorselessly around her, drawing its coils tighter and tighter until she shivered. She had to say something to break the silence. 'How long will you be away?' she croaked, horrified at how husky her voice sounded. She cleared her throat and gulped at her coffee, hoping that Lyall would think that she had a crumb stuck in her throat.

'A couple of weeks,' he said. 'Maybe three.'

There was another agonising silence. Jane clutched her hands around her mug and stared desperately ahead but it was like trying to get a compass to point south instead of north. No matter how hard she tried, her attention veered back to where Lyall was sitting still and silent at the end of the sofa.

'Are you really going to marry Alan Good?' he spoke suddenly out of the shadows.

It was too late to pretend. Jane turned to face him at last, but she couldn't read his expression. 'No,' she said.

The lamplight caught Lyall's face as he leant forward and set his mug on the carpet. 'Good,' he said, and then glanced at Jane. 'Then you won't be too upset to know that Dimity was doing a pretty good job of consoling him for your absence last weekend?'

Jane lost her shyness in astonishment. 'Dimity?' she echoed. 'I thought Dimity spent last weekend with you?'

'With me?' It was his turn to look surprised. 'What on earth made you think that?'

'She did,' said Jane simply.

Lyall's brows drew together. 'I certainly saw her. She was desperate to discuss some designs, so I arranged to meet her at the manor on Saturday morning, and since it was lunchtime when we'd finished we went down to the pub; but that was all. I'd hardly call a meeting and a drink in the pub spending the weekend together, would you?'

'You mean you didn't see her that night?'

'No.' Lyall looked at Jane and then away. 'For one reason or another, I decided to go back to London. I left Dimity and Alan arranging to go out to dinner together.' He hesitated. 'Do you mind?'

'About Alan?' Jane shook her head. If anything, she felt giddy with relief. 'No. Do you?'

There was no mistaking his surprise at her question. 'Why on earth should *I* mind?'

'Dimity's very pretty,' she muttered, and Lyall's smile gleamed suddenly through the darkness.

'Yes, she is,' he agreed. 'But you know better than anyone, Jane, that I like a very different kind of girl.'

The silence stretched and twanged between them. Jane's mouth dried, and her pulse boomed in her ears as she fumbled her mug on to the coffee-table. 'I—er—I'd better let you get to bed if you've got an early start,' he stammered, and got up on to legs that were suddenly unsteady.

'Yes.' Lyall's face was unreadable as he rose to his feet as well.

They faced each other through the soft light. The lamp drew a glow over Jane's cheek, just catching the curve of her mouth and the wide gleam of her eyes. She cleared her throat and smiled nervously.

'Well . . . thank you for a lovely meal.'

She had to pass him to get to the door. Lyall stood back to let her go, and made no move to touch her, only spoke her name in a low, urgent voice as she stepped past him. 'Jane?'

'Yes?' she croaked.

'Don't you want to know why I didn't stay in Penbury last weekend?'

Jane swallowed. 'Why?'

'Because you weren't there,' he said slowly. 'I only went down in the hope that I might see you. You wouldn't talk to me on the phone, so I thought I might have a better chance of explaining if only I could see you face to face. But when I got there you'd gone, and the village felt empty without you.' Lyall paused and looked down into her face. 'That's when I decided that I might as well give up. I went back to London and told myself that I wasn't going to waste any more time thinking about you. And then you came today . . .'

CHAPTER NINE

LYALL trailed off, as if remembering how he had felt when he had seen her sitting by the pool, clutching the newspaper in front of her in an unsuccessful attempt to hide. 'And then you came,' he said again, his voice very deep and low, 'and I realised that I *couldn't* stop thinking about you, no matter how hard I tried.'

The last breath eked slowly out of Jane's lungs. She couldn't speak, couldn't move, could only stare back at Lyall while his voice reverberated through her and the look in his eyes squeezed her heart.

'I'd really like to kiss you goodnight,' he went on in the same deep, mesmerising voice. 'But after last time I promised myself that I wouldn't kiss you again—unless you kissed me first, that is.'

And all at once it was easy. The last fragile link holding Jane above temptation cracked and crumbled before the slow, slamming assault of her heart, and she succumbed painlessly, discovering that giving in felt not shameful or alarming, but utterly right. The twanging tension and the jittery nerves dissolved along with her resistance and she drew a deep breath of release.

'I see,' she said, but a smile hovered around her mouth, and she stepped up to him, laying her hands flat against his chest. 'Does that mean that you'd like me to kiss *you*?'

'Yes, please,' said Lyall unsteadily.

He stood quite still as Jane lifted her hands to his face, tracing his cheek and jaw with light, tantalising fingers, feeling the rough, male texture of his skin. Slowly, she

154

let them drift round to his hair so that she could pull
his head down to hers. His mouth was only a breath
away. Her gaze lingered lovingly on it as she savoured
the anticipation of kissing him at last and the wonder
of not having to pretend any more.

She looked deep into his eyes for one long, quiet
moment, and then she closed the gap and pressed her
lips tenderly against his. Pleasure at the warm, firm feel
of them seared her, but Lyall made no move to respond.
Couldn't he feel the electric thrill that ran between them
whenever they touched?

A terrible doubt seized Jane. What if he *had* just meant
a goodnight kiss? Faltering, she began to withdraw, only
to find herself trapped in strong arms as Lyall grinned
wickedly down at her.

'You didn't really think I was going to let you go, did
you, Jane?' he teased.

'Oh, you——!' Relief warred with indignation in
Jane's face, but she really didn't mind. Laughing, she
let herself be caught back against him, and this time it
was Lyall who kissed her, a deep, blissful kiss where the
teasing and the laughter soon faded into something far
more powerful that leapt into life and burned high between them.

Murmuring her name between kisses, Lyall drew her
back down to the sofa and pulled her on to his lap. Jane
sank against him, wrapping her arms around his neck
as he gathered her closer, kissing him back with a passion
that grew with every moment.

His fingers were at the buttons of her shirt, and she
sat back slightly to make it easier for him, pulling the
material free of her jeans with hands that shook with
desire. When he brushed the shirt aside and slid his hands
over her skin, she gasped at the jagged wrench of excitement. They were so warm, so sure, curving over her

breasts and insistent against her back, tracing a line of fire down her spine...

Jane arched into him. She was spinning with pleasure, and her hands clutched at his hair as if he was her only anchor to reality. Their kisses grew hungrier, more desperate, every sense clamouring with need, every inch of her ablaze with feeling.

Surfacing for breath at last, Jane trailed her lips along his jaw. 'I thought you wanted an early night?' she whispered, her voice ragged with desire as Lyall slid the shirt from her shoulders so that he could look at her. Her skin was luminous in the lamplight, and although his voice held a low ripple of laughter his hands were unsteady as he caressed her. 'That would be the sensible thing to do,' he agreed, 'but right now I don't feel like being very sensible, do you?'

Jane shuddered as he played his fingers around her breast. 'No,' she gasped. 'Not this time.'

Lyall tipped her gently off his lap and stood up, silencing her mumbled protests with a kiss before pulling her through to his bedroom. 'Do you realise that we've never once made love on a bed before?' he asked, expertly divesting her of what remained of her clothing.

'Haven't we?' Breathless beneath the devastating assault of his hands, Jane hardly knew what she was saying, and it took all her concentration to unbutton his shirt and unfasten his trousers as they progressed between kisses towards the bed.

'No.' Lyall pulled her down and rolled her beneath him to blizzard kisses along the pure sweep of her shoulders, down to the swell of her breasts. 'And I remember every time.'

Jane ran her hands over his bare skin, exulting in the sleek, steely strength of his body. 'Do you? Do you really?'

His mouth drifted back up to her throat. 'Yes,' he murmured against her lips. 'Do you?'

How could she lie when her bones were dissolving beneath his touch and his kisses were spiralling her back to a time when nothing had existed but the wild pulse of longing and nothing had mattered as long as they were together?

'Yes,' she said softly. 'I remember too.'

Lyall lifted his head at that and braced himself with his arms on either side of her so that he could look deep into her eyes. No words were spoken; none was needed. And then the past and the present blended into one as he lowered his body on to hers and their lips met in a kiss that acknowledged just how great was the desire that burned between them.

He explored her body with excruciating slowness at first, possessing her with hard hands, letting his lips linger, tasting the sweet, silken warmth of her until she was molten beneath him, her blood running like fire, the very core of her aflame with need. The muscles in his back flexed and rippled as her hands moved over him lovingly in turn, sliding down his flanks, touching him as she had dreamed of touching him for so long, and their kisses grew fierce with a gathering rush of urgency.

Jane was spinning, soaring, her senses swirling up to another plane where there was only Lyall, his mouth and his hands and the hard promise of his body, and she sobbed his name as she dug her fingers into his shoulders.

'Lyall...'

'Soon,' he promised, and his lips drifted up her stomach, grazing her breasts with a murmured endearment and kindling a shuddering trail of fire up her throat to find her mouth once more as, with a shaft of exquisite pleasure, he moved over her and in her.

Jane gasped in glorious release and wrapped herself around him, instinctively urging him on as together they

were borne on a tide of intense, inexpressible feeling t
the very brink of sensation. For an eternal moment the
hesitated there before leading each other on and ove
and down into an incandescent burst of ecstasy that lef
them awed and breathless in each other's arms as the
sank slowly, slowly down into the afterglow.

Their ragged breathing was the only sound in the diml
lit room. Lyall lay heavily on her, and Jane found tha
there were tears sliding down her face.

'What is it?' he whispered, turning his head to kis
her and discovering her wet cheeks.

Unable to explain, Jane only shook her head an
smiled at him through her tears. Lyall wiped her cheek
tenderly with his thumb and kissed her very gently o
the mouth. 'I know,' he said.

They were still entwined as he rolled on to his back
taking Jane with him. She rested her cheek against hi
shoulder and wondered why she had resisted this for s
long. Wasn't this where she belonged, fitted comfortabl
into his side, feeling his chest rise and fall, listening t
him breathe?

His hand smoothed up and down the arm that la
across his chest in an unthinking caress and he sighed
a deep, slow, contented sigh. 'Jane...'

'Mmm?'

Smiling, he kissed her hair. 'Just...*Jane*,' he sai
softly, and he held her close as she fell asleep to th
steady beat of his heart.

When Lyall kissed her awake, he was fully dressed an
outside the rosy flush of dawn lingered in the lightenin
sky.

'The car's waiting downstairs,' he said as Jane stirre
and stretched. She smiled sleepily up at him, and h
caught his breath. 'Don't look like that, Jane, or I'
never get to Frankfurt!'

Her smile faded as she remembered. 'I wish you didn't have to go.'

'Come with me.' Lyall leant over and kissed her, and she linked her hands around his neck to pull him closer. 'I mean it. Come with me, Jane.'

'I can't,' she said, half laughing, half torn by temptation. 'I haven't got anything with me.'

'We can buy whatever you need,' he urged.

'You can't buy a passport,' said Jane regretfully. 'And even if it were possible I couldn't just take off and leave the firm just now... We happen to have an important contract to fulfil!'

'So you do!' Lyall smiled, but then his expression grew serious. 'We haven't had a chance to talk, and there's so much I need to say to you. Now I'm going to be away for a couple of weeks.' He ran his fingers through his hair. 'I'd cancel the trip, but it's taken us years to set this up. I can't let everyone down now.'

Jane laid her palm against his cheek. 'Of course you can't. We can talk when you get back.' She kissed him gently. 'You'll always know where to find me.'

'I suppose so.' Smoothing the honey-coloured hair away from her face, Lyall gave her one last, lingering kiss then disentangled himself reluctantly. 'I'd better go. Judith's coming in later to pick up some papers, so she can give you a lift back to the van. It won't be until later, though, so you can go back to sleep now.'

A last, loving touch to her hair and he was gone. Jane lay back against the pillows and stretched luxuriously. She had forgotten that it was possible to feel this contented, this complete. Memories of the night before kept rising like slow bubbles to the surface, breaking into spreading ripples of happiness.

She was just drifting off to sleep again when the phone rang in the other room. Her first thought was that it must be Lyall, ringing from the car. Who else would be phoning at this time of the morning? Suddenly desperate just to hear his voice, she pulled on a towelling robe that hung behind the door, but the phone stopped as she rushed through, and she saw that it had switched automatically through to a fax machine.

Wondering if it was some urgent message that she should try to get through to Lyall somehow, Jane craned her neck to read the text as the paper oozed out of the machine. It was from Australia, which explained the odd timing, but it didn't seem to have 'urgent' written all over it, so presumably Judith would deal with it when she came.

Disappointed that it hadn't been Lyall, but too awake to go back to sleep now, Jane waited until the last page came through and then carried the fax over to where a pile of papers sat on a desk. She was about to drop it on to the top when her eye was caught by the message which lay just beneath, and her hand froze. What was this about Penbury Manor? Laying the Australian fax to one side, she picked up the piece of paper and as she read it the glow of happiness drained from her face.

It was a message from Judith dated over a week ago.

Dennis Lang phoned and needs to talk to you urgently before you go to Japan. He has been looking at various properties to replace Penbury Manor and has two which seem suitable—he is sending you details—but needs a decision from you as to whether you want to stop work at Penbury immediately or wait until the end of the first phase.

At the bottom, Lyall had scribbled Judith a note.

Spoke to Dennis this afternoon. He's going to negotiate for Dilston House and will be in touch with you later about contracts for renovation. Once we know we've got it, I'll sort things out with the Penbury contractors. Until then, please keep change of plans confidential.

Jane read the message twice, then replaced it very carefully on to the pile of papers and covered it with the fax. A change of plans? Why hadn't he told her? Or was she, after all, just a contractor who was going to be 'sorted out'?

No, she wasn't that, not after last night. Jane thought of the look in Lyall's eyes as he'd said goodbye and was reassured, but her happiness had cracked, just a little. Battling the lurking sense of unease, she showered and dressed and let herself out of the flat without waiting for Judith. It was still very early and the streets were quiet, but she managed to find a taxi to take her back to the Multiplex headquarters so that she could pick up the van.

The doubt grew as she drove down the motorway. Why had Lyall changed his mind about Penbury Manor? He *knew* how much that contract meant to Makepeace and Son. Had it been his way of punishing her for that argument? Had he taken her at her word when she had told him to leave her and Penbury alone?

Jane tried desperately to shore up her crumbling happiness with memories of the night before, but it was hopeless. That uncompromising message seeped relentlessly through her mind, like water trickling through sand. She couldn't tell the men that their bright future had disappeared until Lyall deigned to tell her himself, but how was she to carry on pretending that everything was all right?

And then an even worse thought occurred to her. Had Lyall's offer of an advance been intended as a sop to his conscience, a pay-off against the time when neither she nor Makepeace and Son would have a place in his life? If it had, what did that say about last night?

Jane drove straight to the manor, where the men un-
loaded the fireplaces. Wandering around to check up on
the progress afterwards, she ended up in Lyall's bedroom.
She remembered standing there by the window with him,
remembered the way he had smiled and asked her if it
was the kind of room she would like to go to bed in.
The sense of his presence was so strong that Jane almost
turned to see if he was behind her, and her eyes stung
with sudden tears. She missed him with a physical ache.
If only he were here. If only she could lean against him
and feel his arms close around her and listen to him explaining that it was all a ghastly mistake.

She ran her hand along the windowsill. It *was* a
mistake. It had to be. She had completely misunderstood that note and it served her right for reading something that was none of her business. This time, she told
herself, she would trust Lyall.

Dimity was coming up the main staircase as Jane made
her way slowly down. 'Oh, *hi!*' she cried. Only Dimity
could stretch two letters into sixteen syllables.

Suppressing a sigh, Jane said hello. In spite of what
Lyall had told her about Dimity and Alan, she was pri-
vately convinced that the other girl was still haunting the
manor in the hope of seeing Lyall himself. 'Up here
again? You're very conscientious.'

'I was just having a last look around,' Dimity explained, with an exaggerated sigh of nostalgia.

Jane went very still. 'What do you mean?'

'Hasn't Lyall told you about his change of plans?'
asked Dimity artlessly.

'Not specifically.' Jane's voice seemed to be coming
from a long way off.

'Perhaps I'd better not say any more...'

'I gather this change of plans means that Multiplex
isn't going ahead with its plans for Penbury Manor?'

Jane said harshly, and although Dimity spread her hands apologetically her green eyes were smug.

'I thought Lyall would have told you,' she said sweetly. 'After all, the change affects you more than anyone else, doesn't it?'

'It would have been nice if I'd been told, yes.'

'Lyall gave me a hint when he was down for the weekend.' Dimity patted her curls with an ill-disguised smirk. 'Of course, I was *horrified* to hear that he'd decided that another house would suit his plans better, but he *assured* me that my place in his plans wouldn't change at all.' The green eyes were complacent as she glanced at Jane's stony face. 'Dilston House looks lovely, but there's something special about Penbury, isn't there?'

'Yes.' Jane was beginning to feel sick. 'Does that mean you'll be doing the interior design at their new centre?'

'Oh, yes,' said Dimity, as if it had always been a foregone conclusion. 'It means that the work I've already put in here is wasted, of course, but Lyall has *promised* that I'll be compensated.' She leant forward confidingly. 'I *gather* they're planning to use all the same contractors, but it might be a bit different for you. Dilston's near Oxford, and that would be too far for your men to go every day, wouldn't it? They're more likely to employ a firm of local builders. It's *such* a shame,' she went on with a patronising look. 'Your men have been doing a *super* job, but perhaps the new owners here will want to keep you on to finish the renovations?'

'Perhaps,' said Jane bleakly. Somehow she managed to say goodbye and get herself across the hall and out to the van where she sat for long minutes, staring blindly ahead of her.

So it was true. Lyall was leaving Penbury as abruptly as he had returned, and she was the only one he hadn't bothered to tell.

He rang the following morning, just as she was about to leave for the office. Jane knew it would be him before she even picked up the phone. Inside she felt bruised and raw after a sleepless night, but outwardly she was utterly, frighteningly composed. She felt as if she was encased in an icy grip that was tightening inexorably around her until it was an effort to breathe.

When the phone rang, she didn't even jump. 'At last!' Lyall's voice radiated warmth from the other side of the world. 'I thought I'd never get a chance to ring you. How are you?'

'Fine,' said Jane, who had never felt worse.

'Are you sure?' He was obviously puzzled. 'You don't sound like the girl I left yesterday morning—or is it just the line?'

Jane's fingers tightened around the receiver. 'I think it would be best if we forgot about that night.'

There was a brief, stunned silence. 'Forget about it?' Lyall echoed incredulously. 'What are you talking about, Jane? How can you ask me to forget about a night like that?'

'I'd rather pretend that it never happened.'

'But *why*?' he exploded. 'What is it? What's the matter?'

Everything. 'Nothing,' said Jane. Her throat was so tight that she couldn't manage to say any more.

'Don't give me that! One day you're kissing me goodbye like you never want to let me go, and the next you're carrying on like a total stranger. Why are you suddenly trying to pretend that night meant nothing to you?'

'I'm not pretending,' she said, astonished by the steadiness in her own voice. She couldn't ask him why he hadn't told her about his change of plans. What would be the point? She had learnt all she needed to know from Dimity, and she didn't think her control would last.

'Why sleep with me at all, then?' demanded Lyall, hurt and anger boiling in his voice. 'You didn't have to kiss me. You didn't have to make love.'

'What did you expect me to do when you'd just offered to advance me all that money?'

As soon as the words were out, Jane knew that she had gone too far. There was a long, dangerous silence, and when Lyall spoke his tone slashed her from thousands of miles away. 'How dare you?' he said with such a deadly lack of emphasis that in spite of herself Jane flinched. 'You knew perfectly well that money had nothing to do with what happened between us.'

'It did for me,' she said, knowing that the only way to get through this was to convince him that she had never loved him.

'You kept saying that you'd changed,' said Lyall contemptuously. 'But until now I hadn't realised how much!'

Jane's face was white and she was feeling sick, but she made no attempt to explain herself. She could hear the bitterness and pain in his voice, but why should she make things easy for him? Lyall always wanted everything on his own terms. He had obviously been planning a nice reminiscent affair which would have ended whenever he chose to tell her that he was dumping her along with Makepeace and Son, and he didn't like it when the boot was on the other foot. She could have told him why she had changed so drastically, but with the prospect of laying off the men who had worked so loyally for her over the years hanging over her head Jane didn't feel like giving Lyall that comfort.

'Now you know,' she said.

'I'm surprised you didn't ask for the money before I left,' sneered Lyall. 'I'll get Dennis to send you a cheque tomorrow—or do girls like you prefer cash?'

'A cheque will be fine,' said Jane tonelessly.

'Tell me,' he went on, his voice cold and savage. 'Did you demand money from Alan for the use of that lovely body of yours, Jane? Did he get charged at the same rate, or did I get a discount for regular custom over the years?'

Jane closed her eyes in anguish, but she had started this and she would have to finish it. 'Alan would never need to buy a woman,' she managed with difficulty. 'Any girl would be glad to find a good, kind man like him.'

'So you were lying when you said you weren't going to marry him?' Lyall gave a jeering laugh at his own naïveté. 'But I don't even need to ask, do I? It was all a lie!'

'I did tell him that I wouldn't marry him, but I've changed my mind,' said Jane, feeling as if she was trapped in some nightmare. 'I used to take his reliability and integrity and good, plain niceness for granted, but meeting you again has changed that.'

'And now you're going to try and grab him back out of Dimity's clutches?'

'If he'll have me.'

'Don't you think a nice, reliable chap like Alan deserves an equally nice girl?' he asked insultingly. 'He'd be better off with Dimity than with a girl like you with no shame and no heart! Because you don't care about anyone but yourself, do you, Jane? You never have and you never will.'

Pain clawed at Jane's heart and the tight band of misery around her throat was making it hard to talk. 'I care about lots of people,' she said dully, thinking about Dorothy and the men who looked to her to preserve their livelihoods. 'I just don't care about you.'

Her lie echoed along the line to Japan. In sudden panic, Jane wanted to call it back, but it was too late. 'I see,' said Lyall in a flat, cold voice. 'In that case, there doesn't seem to be much more to say, does there?'

The tears were sliding down Jane's cheeks, but she mustn't let him hear her cry. 'No,' she said, and her heart cracked and splintered into a thousand pieces as she put down the phone.

The next three weeks were like living a nightmare. Jane struggled under the oppressive weight of misery which seemed to be crushing her on every side, making it hard to move, an effort even to breathe. Dorothy saw that something was very wrong, but Jane refused to talk about it. There was no point in worrying anyone else until Multiplex had confirmed that it was cancelling the contract, and in the meantime she just had to keep it all to herself.

The strain soon began to show. She grew thin and gaunt, and the eyes which had always been so clear and grey now held a haunted look. It was a struggle to try and behave normally when she ached with the memories of Lyall's loving and the knowledge of Lyall's betrayal.

During the day, Jane clung to her routine. She spent as much time as she could in the office, trying to distract herself with work, but nothing made the nights any better. She would lie in bed and fight to remember the contract, the lost hopes, but the anger she sought only drained away in the face of other memories that slid insidiously into her mind, memories of Lyall's lean, hard body, of his sure hands and the enchantment they had shared. Every night she relived each kiss, each touch, and her heart would break anew at the thought that she would never know such joy again.

Lyall sent her a cheque, just as he had said he would. He had written it on his personal account and scrawled across a Multiplex compliment slip was a simple, insulting message: 'For services rendered.' Jane's mouth twisted, and she tore the cheque slowly and deliberately into tiny pieces.

Kit's letter arrived the next day. She should have suspected something when she saw that he'd bothered to send her more than his usual scrappy postcard, but she was so desperate for something to take her mind off Lyall that she pounced on it as it fell through the letter-box and took it into the office to read.

For once Kit had found plenty to say, and he left the bombshell until last. Jane read the letter all the way through three times and then dropped her head into her hands.

'What on earth's the matter?' Dorothy exclaimed in concern as she came in with a pile of letters to find Jane still sitting there numbly. Dropping the letters on to the desk, she put a plump arm around Jane's shoulders. 'Is it Lyall?'

Jane shook her head. This would be the end of Makepeace and Son, but Lyall's name still had the power to make her flinch. She sat back and let Kit's letter fall wearily to the desk once more. 'It's Kit. Carmelita's pregnant and imminent fatherhood has given Kit a sense of responsibility at last. He's decided to settle down and make a go of things in Argentina, so he wants to sell his half of Makepeace and Son to raise enough capital to start his own business out there.' In typical Kit fashion, he had scribbled the request as a breezy postscript.

'Can you afford to buy him out?' asked Dorothy, immediately practical, but Jane had already thought of that.

'There's no way. Even if I sold the house, I wouldn't have enough to give Kit a fair price for his half of the firm, and if we lose that capital we'll just collapse.'

Dorothy looked worried. 'Can't you tell Kit that it's just not possible at the moment?'

'It's his inheritance,' said Jane drearily. 'I've got no right to refuse it to him. Besides, he'll need that money now if he wants to get a business going by the time the baby arrives.'

'What are you going to do?'

Jane's shoulders slumped. 'I don't know... I could go and see the bank, I suppose, but they're more likely to call in their loan than extend it. I'll try and sell Kit's share, but no one in their right mind wants to invest in building companies at the moment.' She could have added that even if anyone was interested they would soon change their mind as soon as they heard that Lyall was about to cancel the contract, but Dorothy had enough to worry about at the moment. 'If that doesn't work, I'm afraid I'll have to put the whole firm on the market.'

Only now did Jane realise how much Makepeace and Son meant to her. She had taken on the responsibility for her father's sake and, as the years had passed, going back to horticulture had dwindled into little more than a dream. The prospect of the Penbury Manor contract had changed all that. Suddenly it had been possible to imagine the financial security that would enable her to get in a manager so that she could go back to doing what she really wanted to do. Selling Makepeace and Son would mean the same thing, Jane knew, but handing a flourishing firm over to a manager was a very different thing from having to admit that she had failed everybody who had worked for her so loyally. And while failure might mean freedom, what use would freedom be without Lyall? Freedom now meant not the opportunity to pick up her career in horticulture, but simply the emptiness of a life without him. Makepeace and Son was all Jane had left, and she wasn't going to give it up without a fight.

CHAPTER TEN

THE next day Jane put on her best cerise suit and went in to see the bank manager. He was as discouraging as she had expected, but he did grudgingly agree to let her know if he heard of anyone wanting to buy into a building firm, and with that Jane had to be satisfied.

She left feeling depressed. On her way back to the van, she saw Alan on the other side of the road, and stopped, wondering if she should talk to him. She hadn't heard from him since she had gone away for that weekend and she hoped he wasn't still feeling hurt. But Alan didn't even notice her. He was holding out his arms and, turning her head curiously, Jane saw Dimity tripping towards him, afloat with the usual ethereal costume and long curls bouncing around her winsome face. She threw herself into Alan's arms and they exchanged a long, passionate kiss in the middle of the pavement.

Jane smiled wryly and carried on. Clearly Alan had allowed himself to be consoled. He and Dimity seemed a most unlikely combination, but if Dimity could make the staid Alan forget himself so far as to kiss like that in public then perhaps they belonged together after all. They said that opposites attracted: look at her and Lyall. They were as different as could be and yet when they had made love none of the differences seemed to matter...

The mere thought of Lyall was enough to make Jane catch her breath in pain, and she forced herself to think about the prospects for Makepeace and Son instead as she drove glumly back to the office. Dorothy put the phone down hurriedly as she went in, but Jane was too despondent to notice her secretary's rather guilty expression.

'He wasn't very hopeful,' she said when Dorothy asked how she had got on with Derek Owen, the bank manager. 'He said he'd put the word around that I'm looking for a new partner, but everyone's been struggling as much as we have. I can't see anyone doing more than thinking about it.'

'Something'll turn up,' said Dorothy cheerfully, and Jane didn't have the heart not to agree, although she couldn't think why her secretary was being so positive. It was impossible to imagine ever feeling positive about anything ever again.

She was wrong. Two days later the bank manager rang and asked her to come in as he had 'a proposition' to put to her. Warning herself not to get her hopes up, Jane climbed back into her suit. To her astonishment, the manager came out wreathed in smiles, and his greeting was positively avuncular. Jane's puzzlement deepened to suspicion. It wasn't like him to be friendly.

'Come in, come in, Miss Makepeace,' he smarmed. 'I think we may safely say that your problem is solved.'

'It *is*?' Jane could hardly believe her ears as he ushered her into his office. 'Do you mean you'll extend my loan?'

'Er, not quite that, no, but someone has expressed an interest in buying a half-share in your company.'

Jane sat down rather abruptly in a chair. 'Who?'

'I'm afraid I can't tell you that,' he said smoothly. 'The enquiry came from someone who specifically asked not to be identified.'

'But they'll have to identify themselves eventually, surely?'

'Not necessarily. All arrangements would be made through us, and the deal would be dependent on continuing anonymity. Our client isn't interested in the day-to-day running of the firm. That would remain entirely in your hands and the buyer would simply be a sleeping partner.'

'I don't understand,' said Jane helplessly. 'What's the point of buying half the firm if you don't want anything to do with it?'

'Our client sees it purely in investment terms,' he explained, and she shook her head as if dazed.

'Are you sure this is a serious offer? It sounds too good to be true!'

The bank manager looked offended. 'I should hardly be wasting your time and mine if it weren't a serious offer,' he pointed out. 'It is, of course, entirely up to you whether you decide to accept it or not,' he added pompously, 'but I should warn you that you are unlikely to get another one like it.'

'I realise that,' said Jane. 'I just wish I knew who it was, even if it's only to thank them. Can't you even give me a hint?'

'I'm afraid not. That would go entirely against our client's instructions.' He looked Jane over as if considering that she hardly deserved such an unexpected stroke of luck. 'Do you wish some time to consider the offer?'

'Does a drowning man take time to consider a lifebelt?'

'I take it, then, that you wish to accept the terms of our client's offer?'

'Yes,' said Jane. 'I accept.'

It was all very strange, she thought, rushing back to tell Dorothy the good news. This anonymous partner of hers hadn't asked for any details or shown any interest in the accounts. She supposed that she should have mentioned the prospect of losing the Penbury Manor contract, but it had all happened so fast. The bank manager had said that he would have the papers ready for her to sign the next week, and if his client was prepared to take the risk, who was she to stop him?

Dorothy was pleased but oddly unsurprised by the news. 'I told you something would turn up,' she said. 'Perhaps when this worry about Kit is out of the way you'll be able to concentrate on... other things.'

Jane didn't want to think about 'other things'. It meant lying awake at night with her body aching for Lyall. It meant her heart cracking painfully every time she went up to the manor or thought about how he smiled or remembered how she quivered whenever he touched her. Over and over again Jane asked herself how she could have been stupid enough to fall in love with Lyall twice. She had *known* what he was like. Hadn't he hurt her enough the first time round? She cursed herself for ever having listened to Judith, for letting herself believe in him, but it didn't stop her jumping every time the phone rang, or looking every time she drove back to her lonely house to see whether he was waiting for her by the door.

He must have been back from Japan at least a week, she calculated, but it was never him at the end of the phone, and her doorstep remained obstinately empty. Jane told herself that she only wanted to see him so that she could prove to him how well she was surviving without him. She wanted him to know that it would take more than his changing his mind to put an end to Makepeace and Son.

With her new anonymous partner, Jane was determined to be stronger than ever before, and she began to look around for new contracts so that she would have something to offer the men when Lyall finally deigned to tell her that the manor deal was off, but it was impossible to make new arrangements when she had no way of knowing exactly when that was going to happen. In the end, she decided to take the bull by the horns and ring up Dennis Lang.

He was charming at first, but evasive when she asked him outright about Multiplex's plans for Penbury Manor, pointing out that the contract had only ever covered the completion of the first phase of works. They would discuss what would happen next when that was complete, and not before.

Frustrated, Jane slammed down the phone. The first phase was nearly over. The new roof was in place, and the manor had been completely rewired and replumbed. All the woodwork had been carefully restored or replaced, and all that was left to do was the plastering, but that shouldn't take long. Makepeace and Son could be out of work in a matter of days. Jane just hoped that her sleeping partner was prepared for a shock.

Kit's share of Makepeace and Son now belonged to a total stranger. The contract had been signed with the bank, and the money transferred straight to Kit in Argentina. Jane had half expected her new partner to spring out of the woodwork as soon as the papers went through, but as the days passed and no one appeared to take an undue interest in the firm's affairs she began to wonder whether her sleeping partner might do as he or she had promised and remain just that.

She should have been grateful that her financial worries were receding. Selling Kit's share of the firm had meant that she no longer needed to contemplate selling Pear Tree Cottage, but it wasn't the comfort she had expected it to be. Nothing was a comfort when there was a cold stone of misery lodged deep and chill inside her. Jane went through the motions, but inside she was numb. The only time she felt anything at all was when she closed her eyes and saw Lyall's blue eyes glinting with laughter, or pictured him as he had looked when he'd lain beside her in the wide bed, his strong, sleek body utterly relaxed and his hands smoothing slowly over her curves.

Then sharp claws of longing would rip savagely through the numbness and rake the dull misery into raw pain.

Every day was a nightmare of talking and smiling and pretending to be normal, but the long, sleepless nights were taking their toll, leaving Jane gaunt and hollow-eyed. The plastering was almost finished and so far she had only been able to find a few small jobs to offer the men when Multiplex cancelled the contract.

The day the plasterers finished, Jane saw them off the premises, locked the door of the manor and made her way wearily back to the office. This, then, was the end. Dorothy wore an air of suppressed excitement that Jane felt quite unable to share as she asked if there were any messages.

'Just one,' said Dorothy with a portentous look.

'What is it?'

'Your anonymous partner is coming to see you here this afternoon! I told him you'd see him at four o'clock,' Dorothy added, delighted at the effect of her announcement.

Jane gathered her wits together. 'Four o'clock? It's ten to four now! I won't be ready for him . . . it *is* a him, is it?'

'It was definitely a male voice.'

'Right.' Jane drew a deep breath. 'I mustn't look flustered. We don't want some man coming in and deciding everything's so chaotic that he needs to start interfering!'

'Here, take these,' said Dorothy, offering her the account books. 'You can pretend to be busy looking through these.'

Jane took the books and opened them at random on her desk. Horrified at her pale reflection in the mirror, she put on some lipstick to draw attention away from the shadows under her eyes and dragged a comb through her fine, shining hair. Then she smoothed down her skirt and sat behind her desk, hoping that she looked more businesslike than she felt.

Mindlessly, she turned over the pages of an account book as she wondered what this new partner would be like. Why was he coming now? Would he want to make any changes? What would he say when he discovered that Lyall was cancelling the contract?

Why did everything always come back to Lyall?

Absorbed in her thoughts and expecting Dorothy to buzz her when the mysterious partner arrived, Jane was utterly unprepared when the door opened and Lyall strolled into her office.

The sight of him stopped her heart. She stared, stunned into frozen immobility until her mind caught up with her eyes and her heart slammed back into life with such a jolt that she had to gasp for breath. It was him. It was really him! Her first reaction was an instinctive, incredulous joy just to see Lyall standing there, tall and dark and glinting-eyed, the impact of his presence somehow even more immediate than usual. The sheer excitement must have blazed in her face, for Lyall had taken a step forward before Jane remembered what he had done and pushed back her chair to leap defensively to her feet.

'Wh-what do you want?' she stammered, still shocked by his sudden appearance and appalled at the treacherous way her heart was behaving.

Lyall looked composed in comparison, but then he had the advantage of surprise. 'I wanted to see you,' he said, as if it were the most natural thing in the world. Didn't he remember the bitter words they had exchanged last time they had spoken?

Jane wished that she hadn't got up. Her knees were shaking so much, she was afraid that she would collapse in a messy puddle at his feet, and she leant against the desk, resting her hands on the top for extra support.

'Dorothy shouldn't have let you in,' she said as steadily as she could when her heart was still boomeranging wildly around her chest.

'I persuaded her that you wanted to see me too,' said Lyall calmly.

'Well, I don't,' said Jane, gathering confidence from the fact that between them the desk and her legs were somehow continuing to hold her upright. 'I'm expecting an extremely important visitor any minute, so you'll have to leave.'

Lyall smiled that smile that never failed to catch at her breath. 'I'm gratified to hear that you think I'm so important, Jane.'

'What are you talking about?' Jane looked at him blankly, and he shook his head at her obtuseness.

'Dear Jane! Why do you think I'm here?'

'I don't *know*——' She broke off as an appalling thought struck her. '*You're* not my sleeping partner?'

He grinned at her aghast expression. 'I thought you would have guessed before now.'

Jane opened her mouth, tried to think of something to say, and closed it again. 'It was *you*?' she managed eventually.

'Who else?'

'But... but...' Jane's knees gave way at last and she sat down abruptly. She was beginning to wonder if this was all some crazy dream. 'Why, when you're doing your best to ruin us, should you want to invest in Makepeace and Son?'

Lyall calmly came round the desk and propped himself against it so that he could look down into her face. 'What do you mean, *ruin* you?' he asked patiently. 'Why on earth should I want to do that?'

'Oh, I'm sure you don't *want* to,' flared Jane. 'But you're doing it anyway. And you know perfectly well what I mean! Or are you going to try and deny that you're moving your new centre to a house in Oxfordshire?'

He didn't even make a show of trying to deny it. 'Ah...so you know about that, do you?'

'I realise that I wasn't meant to know,' she said coldly. 'I appear to be the only one of your contractors who wasn't.'

'There was a reason for that——' Lyall began, but Jane interrupted him before he had a chance to finish.

'Yes, and I know what it was!'

There was an odd smile at the back of his eyes. 'Do you?'

'It wasn't very hard to guess,' she said bitterly. 'None of the other people who had contracts at Penbury Manor was due to start any work until the second phase, so it was easy to keep them sweet by transferring their contracts to the new centre. None of them needed to be particularly local, but it was different for me, wasn't it?'

'It was always different for you,' Lyall admitted, but instead of looking ashamed of the way he had treated her he wore a suspiciously cheerful expression.

Jane eyed him with deep resentment. How could he sit there coolly admitting his callous lack of concern for her feelings and *still* send her pulse-rate rocketing giddily?

'I wasn't supposed to know in case I pulled the men off the job before the end of the first phase, and you wanted that stage of the renovation finished so that you'd get more money when you sold the manor.'

Her tone was belligerent, but Lyall's look of amusement only deepened. 'You seem very well-informed about all the arrangements, Jane.'

'I met Dimity having a last look around the manor,' she explained tersely. 'She couldn't wait to tell me how involved she was in your new plans.'

'Yes, she's keen, isn't she?' said Lyall thoughtfully. 'She's already been round Dilston House and sent me her first ideas. You may not like Dimity very much, but there's no denying that she's a talented interior designer.'

'Bully for her,' snapped Jane. 'I suppose Dimity's *talent* was the reason you were so keen to keep her informed of developments?'

A smile was twitching at the corner of Lyall's mouth. 'There wasn't much point in her wasting any more of her time at Penbury Manor,' he explained reasonably, and Jane's temper snapped.

'Whereas it was all right for me to waste *my* time?' Her grey eyes were bright with hurt and anger. 'I was just the contractor you were going to "sort out" when you got back from your trip!'

'You were never that, Jane.'

'Wasn't I? That was certainly how you put it to Judith!'

His amusement faded. 'When did I say that?'

Jane didn't quite meet his eyes. 'I saw a note you left for her that morning after...' She didn't want to say after they had made love. 'After you left,' she compromised. 'I know I shouldn't have read it, but a fax came through just after you'd gone, and I was putting it on the pile you'd left for Judith when I saw you'd written her a note about Penbury Manor...so I read it.' She lifted her chin defiantly. 'It made it very clear what you were planning to do.'

'So that was it!' Lyall let out a long breath. 'Jane, why didn't you *ask* me about it?'

'I was going to, but then I met Dimity, and she knew all about it.' Jane looked down at the hands she was gripping together in her lap. 'It was obvious that I was the only one you hadn't bothered to tell.' She tried to sound cool and unconcerned, but the memory of that terrible realisation cracked her voice.

'So when I rang you pretended that you'd only made love to me because of the money?'

'Yes.' Too late, she heard the admission. 'I mean...I wasn't pretending...' She trailed off as Lyall reached down for her hands and pulled her to her feet so that their knees were almost touching. Propped as he was against the desk, their eyes were quite level when she was standing up. Jane's gaze slid frantically away from his and she tried to tug her hands free, but she couldn't break his grip.

'Jane,' he said with a mixture of laughter and despair. 'Why do you think I bought Makepeace and Son anonymously?'

'I can't imagine,' she muttered, still not looking at him. She wished she weren't so excruciatingly aware of his warm, strong fingers around hers, of the nearness of his body, of the fact that she would only have to lean forward a matter of inches to touch his mouth.

'It was the only way you would let me into your life,' he told her.

Jane could feel his eyes on her face, but kept her gaze firmly fixed on the account books which still lay open and unread on the desk. 'Why bother with that when selling the manor was the quickest way to ensure that I'd be *out* of your life?'

'I'm not selling the manor,' said Lyall unexpectedly. Surprise made her lift her eyes to his, and once she was caught by those dark blue depths she couldn't look away. 'At least,' he went on, 'I don't think am.'

'Wh-what are you going to do with it?' Held by his eyes, Jane was having trouble remembering her righteous indignation.

'That depends on you,' he said, a smile lurking in his eyes.

'On me?'

'I thought we could live there,' said Lyall, quite casually. 'You told me ten years ago that it would be a good place to bring up a family, and I can't think of anywhere better. What do you think?'

Jane was incapable of thinking anything. She could only stare into the deep blue eyes and let hope trickle incredulously into her sore heart.

'Of course, if you were telling the truth when you said you didn't care about me, I would sell,' he continued when she didn't say anything, and then the lurking smile had vanished and his eyes were very serious as he tightened his grip on her hands. 'I couldn't bear to live there without you, Jane.'

'What are you saying?' asked Jane slowly, hardly daring to believe, and Lyall rubbed his thumbs lightly over the back of her hands.

'I'm saying that I love you,' he said with a steady look. 'I don't want to lose you again, Jane. I want to be able to reach out at night and touch you. I want to see you smile in the mornings. I want to be able to come home every evening and know that you'll be there. I want to marry you.'

'But . . . you've always said that you never want to get married,' she whispered, still unable to take it all in.

'I've changed my mind,' said Lyall, lifting her hands to kiss first one and then the other. 'I've changed my mind about a lot of things since I came back to Penbury. I've learnt that the past is always a part of you, that you can't deny it, or run away from it. Some time or other it has to be faced. I thought that I'd left it all behind when I left Penbury, but I hadn't. I'd just tried to forget it, just as I tried to forget you, and I nearly succeeded. Nearly, but not quite. Because whenever I met a girl I'd find that her eyes weren't quite as clear as yours, and her hair wasn't quite as soft, and she didn't smile quite the way you did. I talked about freedom because it was easier to do that than to admit that my parents' marriage had made *me* scared of marriage and to accept that I hadn't stayed and fought for the only girl I'd ever really wanted.'

Tenderly, he smoothed a strand of hair away from Jane's face. 'I told myself I enjoyed my independent existence, but coming back to Penbury changed that, too. I began to imagine having a place where I belonged, a place I could call home, and the more I imagined it, the more I associated that place with you. That's why I asked Dennis to look around for another site for the research centre. I wanted Penbury to be a home for us both, but then we had that argument in the woods and you refused to speak to me, and I began to think that I was wasting my time dreaming. That was when you came up to London, and suddenly the dream was real.' He paused, and his eyes held an expression that Jane had never seen there before... Could it really be anxiety? His voice was very low. 'Did you really mean it when you said that that night we shared meant nothing to you, Jane?'

Jane could feel her heart swelling with a wonderful, glorious, incredible happiness, bursting apart the tight bands of misery that had been clamped around it for so long. She shook her head slowly. 'No,' she said softly, and curled her fingers around his. 'There was only ever you.'

'You don't want a nice, safe, steady husband?'

'No,' she smiled. 'I want you.'

A smile started at the back of Lyall's eyes and spread slowly over his face. 'You love me?' He wanted her to say it out loud, to convince him.

It was wonderful to be honest at last. 'Desperately,' she said.

'And you'll marry me?'

'Yes,' said Jane, and joy spilled through her in a golden rush as he drew her towards him. 'Oh, yes, yes, I will!'

Lyall released her hands to slide his arms around her and gather her against the hard security of his body, and she melted joyfully into his kiss. It was bliss to be able to kiss him back, to put her arms around his neck and hold him close, to touch him and taste him and feel him and know that he loved her.

Giddy with the sudden release from despair, Jane clung to him as they exchanged deep, desperate kisses that banished the last wisps of uncertainty. 'Do you really love me?' she murmured breathlessly at last against his jaw as Lyall held her between his knees and teased his lips down her throat.

He lifted his head at that and smoothed the honey-gold hair behind her ears with hands that were not quite steady. 'Yes,' he said with an intensity that shook her. 'You must believe me, Jane.'

'I do,' she said, and her eyes were clear and shining as she kissed him again. 'I always will.'

Lyall brought her back hard against him and rested his cheek against her hair, smoothing his hand down her back as if he could hardly believe that he held her in his arms again. 'I think I've wanted this ever since I walked on to the terrace at Penbury Manor and saw you standing among the roses. It was as if the last ten years had never happened. I couldn't believe that I'd even pretended to try and forget you, and I was determined to get to know you all over again, but you didn't make it easy for me.'

'I was afraid,' Jane admitted. 'I didn't want to be hurt again. No one had ever made me feel the way you did. I knew how easily I would fall in love with you all over again if I let myself, so I tried everything not to, but it didn't do any good. The truth was that I'd never fallen *out* of love with you.'

'I wish I'd known,' said Lyall, kissing her ear. 'Whenever I kissed you, I thought that you still loved me, but you were so prickly it was impossible to be sure.

After that argument in the woods, I began to suspect that I was just making a monumental fool of myself. You were so insistent that it was Alan you really wanted, and I was furious with myself for wanting you anyway. I wouldn't give up, though. I rang and rang, but you would never talk to me, and it wasn't until I came down for that weekend that I realised how much I would hate Penbury without you. That's when I decided to sell the manor and forget all about you...and then you came up to London and suddenly I was sure that you loved me after all.'

'Why didn't you say anything then?' asked Jane, muffled against his throat.

'I didn't want to rush things. I thought that was the mistake I'd made before, and that we'd do better to start again and get to know each other more slowly. I knew I had to leave early the next morning, and that we wouldn't have a chance to talk properly, so I decided that it would be best if we just said goodnight. I was going to be very sensible—only it didn't quite work out the way I had planned!'

Jane smiled at the memory. 'What made you decide not to be sensible after all?'

'Just the way you looked in the lamplight.' Lyall drifted a finger lovingly down her cheek. 'Just knowing that everything would be all right as long as you were there. I was going to ask you to marry me as soon as I got back, but when I rang you from Japan you'd changed completely. I couldn't believe the things you were saying, and I was devastated. Just when the dream had come true, it was shattered again.'

'I'm sorry,' said Jane, laying her hand against his face. 'I'm so sorry, Lyall...but I was convinced that you were planning to cancel the contract. It wasn't just a case of me feeling as if I'd been used. I really thought you were going to put all the men who work for me out of a job too.'

'I should have told you what I was thinking of, instead of letting you get hold of completely the wrong end of the stick.' Lyall sighed and drew her back against him. 'You'd think we'd have learnt our lesson after last time, wouldn't you?'

Jane held him tightly. 'We've wasted so much time!'

'We'll make up for it,' he said, and they kissed to seal the promise.

Much later, Jane gave a shuddering sigh of happiness and laid her head against Lyall's shoulder. 'How did you find out that I needed a partner?'

'Dorothy told me.'

She pulled away in astonishment. '*Dorothy*?'

'When I'd calmed down a bit, I decided that you had to be lying for some reason,' Lyall explained. 'Whenever I thought about the night we had shared, I knew that you loved me. You would never have slept with me just for money, but I couldn't understand why you should say that you had. There had to be something wrong, so I rang Dorothy to find out what it was. She didn't know, but I took some comfort from the fact that she said you were looking as wretched as I felt, and when you heard from Kit she rang and told me what had happened. I knew how responsible you felt about the firm, so I set up the deal with the bank. At the time I was desperate for any connection with you.'

'But why did you insist on being anonymous?'

'I thought you might refuse if you knew it was me. You have to remember that I was consumed with jealousy imagining that you had made the decision to go back to Alan in spite of what had happened between us. It was only when Dimity came up to London to give me her first sketches for Dilston House and told me that she and Alan were engaged that I let myself hope that everything would work out after all. I decided that I would wait for the work to be finished on the first phase and then come and ask you what I should do with it next. If you really wanted nothing more to do with me, I would put it on the market, but I was pinning everything on the hope that you would say that we should restore the manor together as a home for us and our children.'

Jane subsided blissfully back against him and pretended to consider. 'Does Makepeace and Son still get the contract for the restoration work?' she murmured between kisses.

'Only if you get in a manager,' said Lyall, with the air of one striking a hard bargain. 'We've got a lot of time to catch up on, you and I. I want you with me.'

'And if I agree to your terms, how long is this contract to be binding?' Jane asked, kissing his ear and beginning to work her way tantalisingly back to his mouth until she felt Lyall smile against her lips.

'Forever,' he promised.

EPILOGUE

MULTIPLEX PLC
From the Chairman and Chief Executive

Mrs Jane Harding
Executive Director
Makepeace and Son
Starbridge

Dear Mrs Harding

Further to our recent discussions, I have great pleasure in accepting Makepeace and Son's tender for the final stages of the restoration of Penbury Manor.

Please note that the contract is awarded on condition of your personal attention to me at all times. All building work is to be overseen by your new manager, who will be responsible for the day-to-day running of Makepeace and Son, but you are to take exclusive responsibility for restoring the manor gardens according to your own wishes. However, your primary responsibility will be to liaise closely with me on all aspects of transforming Penbury Manor into a home.

If these terms are agreeable, would you please confirm your acceptance of the contract as soon as possible so that we can ensure that it is legally binding on both sides?

I look forward to continuing our very happy partnership together in a lovely old house.

With love, always

LYALL

Return this coupon and we'll send you 4 Mills & Boon romances and a mystery gift absolutely FREE! We'll even pay the postage and packing for you.

We're making you this offer to introduce you to the benefits of Reader Service: FREE home delivery of brand-new Mills & Boon romances, at least a month before they are available in the shops, FREE gifts and a monthly Newsletter packed with information.

Accepting these FREE books and gift places you under no obligation to buy, you may cancel at any time, even after receiving just your free shipment. Simply complete the coupon below and send it to:

HARLEQUIN MILLS & BOON, FREEPOST, PO BOX 70, CROYDON, CR9 9EL.

No stamp needed

Yes, please send me 4 free Mills & Boon romances and a mystery gift. I understand that unless you hear from me, I will receive 6 superb new titles every month for just £1.99* each postage and packing free. I am under no obligation to purchase any books and I may cancel or suspend my subscription at any time, but the free books and gifts will be mine to keep in any case. (I am over 18 years of age)

2EP5R

Ms/Mrs/Miss/Mr _____

Address _____

_____

_____ Postcode _____

Offer closes 31st January 1996. We reserve the right to refuse an application. *Prices and terms subject to change without notice. Offer only valid in UK and Ireland and is not available to current subscribers to this series. **Readers in Ireland please write to: P.O. Box 4546, Dublin 24.** Overseas readers please write for details.

You may be mailed with offers from other reputable companies as a result of this application. Please tick box if you would prefer not to receive such offers. ☐

MILLS & BOON

Kids & Kisses—where kids and romance go hand in hand.

This summer Mills & Boon brings you Kids & Kisses— a set of titles featuring lovable kids as the stars of the show!

**Look out for
Fire Beneath the Ice by Helen Brooks
in August 1995**

Kids...one of life's joys, one of life's treasures.

Kisses...of warmth, kisses of passion, kisses from mothers and kisses from lovers.

In Kids & Kisses...every story has it all.